A GLIMMER OF SILVER

Juliet Kemp

A Glimmer of Silver
Copyright © 2018 Juliet Kemp

This first edition published 2018 by Book Smugglers Publishing
Astoria (USA) & Cambridge (UK)
www.booksmugglerspub.com

Edited by Ana Grilo & Thea James

978-0-463744-71-0 (Ebook)
978-1-791381-28-8 (Paperback)

Cover Art © by Kristina Tsenova
Cover Design © by GermanCreative Fiverr

Book Design and Ebook Conversion by Thea James

For doop, whose enthusiasm never fails,
nor fails to reassure

I WAS FLOATING ON MY back in Ocean, staring up at the mid-afternoon orange of the sky, when it happened.

At the time, I was busy rejoicing in the fact that this was the third-to-last time I would have to do the mandated hourly communion before I could finally escape. If you pass the Test at twelve, you're deemed to be a potential Communicator, and among other things that means an hour in the water every day listening for Ocean. But if you reach sixteen and Ocean hasn't once spoken to you, they have to let you go. Test or not, you must not really be a Communicator after all, and you can go back to normal life and do whatever it is you want to do.

So I was telling myself, like every day, that I wasn't a Communicator, that I didn't want to be, and that just as long as I didn't hear anything they couldn't make me. After nearly four years of utter silence from Ocean, it seemed pretty unlikely that would change in the next three days, and I was bloody delighted.

Which meant I flailed and very nearly sank alto-gether when I heard something bubbling in my ears.

Everyone who can hear Ocean hears Ocean differently. They think that Ocean is hooking into your mind, like telepathy, rather than doing anything to your ears, so the experience is mediated by your own thought patterns. First Contact happened a hundred or so years ago, a couple of decades after we landed on this planet; Comm Alren says it was quite the surprise to our ancestors. Comm Alren teaches us history, and tells us regularly how important our history with Ocean is. I would say to each xyr own, except that Comm Alren wouldn't extend the same courtesy to me because xe expects me to remember all the tedious rubbish xe spouts during lessons. So screw Comm Alren, and screw all the rest of them.

Anyway. To me, it turned out Ocean was going to sound like bubbling. The bubbling didn't make words, not exactly; I just knew what Ocean was saying. And what Ocean was saying was that someone somewhere was eating fish.

What I should have done, what all the protocols say, is that I should have carried on Communicating, and tried to get Ocean to tell me more about where this was happening, and how long it had been going on for, and how serious a problem it was (but of course it happening at all was serious enough already). What I actually did was, I turned myself front side down and swam for the dock as fast as I could.

Comm Tereth looked at me a bit funny as I scrambled onto the dock—I was getting out early—but I told xem I had a cramp and xe shrugged and let me go and dry off. Thankfully no one else was in the changing room to ask what got me so spooked. Or to guess at what it might have been.

The thing was, if I told them, the Communicators proper, I was sunk. That was what I was supposed to do. I was supposed to tell them that I'd heard Ocean, and that there was a problem. Then they'd send a team to sort the problem out, but also there would be the rejoicing that at last I'd come good. Come good by *their* reckoning, that is. Come very bad indeed by my own.

Two more lousy days, and I'd have been free. I bumped down on to the bench in the changing room, hugged my knees to my chest, and swore as many swears as I could think of.

That was when it occurred to me. I hadn't told Comm Tereth when I got out. I hadn't told anyone, yet. What if… What if I just *didn't* tell anyone? They couldn't *know*, if I didn't tell them. Then I could get out anyway, and I could become a musician like I always wanted to, and I could let my skin go back to normal and stay out of the damn water forever and do my level best to forget the last four years altogether.

That did mean no one would know about the fishing. Eating fish is a serious breach of the Contract, and something would have to be done about it, no question. It would have to be properly investigated and all that. But surely Ocean wasn't just going to tell me about it, some kid who wasn't even a proper Communicator. Surely with something this serious Ocean would tell more than one person. Ocean would be telling everyone, right? So someone else would take the message to the other Communicators, and they'd do the needful. It wouldn't be a problem at all.

I took a deep breath, and headed out of the complex to go home. I'd keep quiet. Two more days and this would all be over.

ONCE I GOT BACK CLOSE to home, I did what I normally do, and went to sit on the edge of the city, kicking my heels over the water. I've always liked the water. Maybe I should have realised that it meant something, before the Test.

Endeavour is the first city we built here. There's no land on Ocean, none at all. It's just Ocean, all the way round. The initial remote Survey showed that; what it didn't pick up, or what the scientists examining the data back on Old Earth didn't realise, is that Ocean is sentient. You might think that a planet with no land at all wouldn't be all that great for land-dwelling humans, but on the flipside, it had water (even if we would have to purify it), oxygen, and the right sort of temperature. What with everything happening to and on Old Earth at the time, people were kind of desperate. So the ship Endeavour set off to bring us (our ancestors) here, and once they got here, they landed it in the sea, took it apart, and built the core of the city out of it.

Where I was sitting was part of the later extension built with bamboo. The first priority after landing was food crops, but the second priority was bamboo, because it grows quickly and makes good raft material. After First Contact and the Contract, bamboo became even more important because our ancestors couldn't eat Ocean's fish any more so they needed more farming space. Ocean is the whole ecosystem; fish and molluscs and water plants and all the other aquatic things that we know next to nothing about because they don't map with Old Earth-style marine life. (I say we don't know much about it. We have scientists who want to find out more, but the Communicators are really strict about the Contract, which makes it hard; and anyway, there's the resources issue, like with everything else.)

Anyway. The point is, all of that, it's all Ocean.

So we can't eat it, because you don't eat sentient beings. Even parts of them.

Endeavour extended outwards, as fast as we could grow bamboo, and then after that there were the floating farms that surround it, and after *that*, they started on the islands. Sometimes you can see the first island, Alicante, on the horizon, if we're at a place where the streams come close to each other. Nothing stays still here; everything follows the currents. I couldn't see it today. The second island was Gennaro. Where "was" is the appropriate word.

After a while, Kira came and joined me, like xe does most every day. Kira and I have been friends since we were tinies. Kira's curvy, and smiles a lot, and has long hair the colour of bamboo that xe plaits back for work-days. I used to have long hair. Well. I *used* to have short hair, because it's very curly and that was easiest, and then I passed the Test, and I started growing it. Communicators all have short hair, very short, because they're going in the water all the time. So, you know, I grew mine. I managed two whole (very aggravating) years before I finally got fed up of having wet hair all the damn time and cut it. Now it sticks out all round my head. Kira said it looked nice when I chopped it, but I think that was just to cheer me up.

Kira is about the only person I was friends with before the Test who was still speaking to me after it. Okay, that's a bit of an exaggeration—they're polite, almost all of them—but Kira's the only one who's actually stayed my *friend*. Passing the Test, and going to Comms Centre every day, marks you out as different, and I don't just mean the skin. It's not surprising that once you become an adult, most Communicators move into the area near the Centre and stay there. It doesn't help the whole "weird" thing, though, when people who aren't Communicators only encounter them when they're arguing about the Contract or conveying Ocean's opinions. Hardly ever, like, just socially, at the neighbourhood composter or the requisition centre. Kid Communicators don't even get the arguments. They just get ignored, even by other kids.

I don't know why they make us still live with everyone else when we're this age, given how totally pointless it is and how we'll all wind up near the Centre in the end anyway. I mean, I'm glad, because I like it where I live, and I wouldn't have wanted to leave my parents when I was twelve. (Not sure I'd mind now.) But I'd miss Kira, if I had to go there. I guess I could still come over here, but it would be different.

But it's okay, because in two lousy days I can go back to being normal. I just need to keep my mouth shut.

I really wanted to tell Kira about what I'd heard. My big secret. That idea felt a bit uncomfortable, though I was sure it would wear off once I was free. But still. It was something I'd never be able to tell anyone, ever, in case they sent me back. Maybe it would help to tell Kira—just Kira, no one else. But what if xe wanted me to go back and tell the Communicators about what I heard? What if xe *insisted*?

So when xe asked how I was doing, I just shrugged.

"How about you?" I asked instead, and Kira started telling me all about this new kid, Leo, from Gennaro, who transferred right after the settlement sank, and how utterly beautiful xe was and so on and so forth. Kira's a hopeless romantic but xe never *talks* to any of xyr crushes, just admires them from afar and tells me all about them. None of them ever seem to see how awesome Kira is.

I used to have a bit of a crush on Kira, but I'm not xyr type at all. I'm totally over it now. I did get a bit bored of hearing about Leo after a while, though, so I interrupted.

"How's work going?"

That started xem off on another topic, waving xyr arms around. Kira's going to be a construction-mechanic, xe's known that since we were little, so that's xyr work assignment. Repairing bits of the city mechanism that need it, keeping the whole thing afloat and working and all that. Really, in the long term, what xe wants is to create *new* islands, new cities. Possibly that's part of why xe's so interested in Leo-from-Gennaro, because maybe Leo knows something about why Gennaro sank. (Unlikely. Very few people are interested in that sort of thing, at least not like how Kira is. I'm not that interested, but I'm interested in Kira being enthusiastic, so I sit and listen.)

"And I'm trying to convince them to let me go out on the retrieval team for Gennaro."

"Wow," I said, sincerely. "That is pretty cool."

Kira shrugged. "Well. It will be if I get to go. It's a really interesting problem, and Stel's starting to think…" Kira stopped, and looked a bit shifty, glancing at me sideways. "Anyway. Stel keeps saying how xe's not sure that I really know enough yet and *if* I work really hard this week…"

"Cos you don't work hard normally," I said, rolling my eyes. "Stel thinks the world of you and you know it."

Kira is a really good mechanic, even just as an apprentice, and everyone, including xyr mentor, Stel, knows it. I wondered, though, what it was xe had been going to say, about Gennaro. I thought for a moment about asking, but best not. I didn't want Kira asking me more things, after all.

"So," Kira said. "I've been holding my thumbs. But I promised I'd go back this evening and do a bit extra." Kira glanced at xyr watch.

"Off you go," I said.

Kira shook xyr head. "Tell me about your day first."

I shrugged in turn. "Nothing to tell. Classes. The mandatory daily hour swimming around waiting for something that everyone knows by now isn't going to happen. Ugh. An hour every damn day for four whole years. How much time have I wasted?" It was an old refrain.

"Two more days to go," Kira said, bumping shoulders with me companionably. "Nearly there."

Kira had always been on my side. I hated not telling xem the truth. Maybe... I could tell xem, after all? Kira, of all people, would understand. Kira knew how I felt. I opened my mouth, but Kira wasn't looking at me.

"Jennery, you know, I'm just so glad you'll be out soon, that you're not going to be one of those stupid Communicators after all."

I closed my mouth again.

"I mean," Kira carried on, "it's just kind of absurd, right? How they run everything?" Xe shook xyr head. "And all this talking to Ocean... That's just weird, right? I'm so glad for you that the test was wrong. Two more days and you're out."

My shoulders had tensed. I didn't want Kira to think I was weird. I would just keep quiet, with Kira same as with everyone else. It was safer that way, anyway. And then I'd be out, like xe said. And yet... Was that really what Kira had thought for the last four years and just not told me until now?

Kira turned to look at me, and I found a smile for xem. Kira had *always* been on my side. It was all fine.

"Did you get a chance to practice at all today?" xe asked.

What I want to do, which Kira knows, and no one else cares about any more, is music. Playing it, writing it, all of it. I was on target for it, when I was younger. Before the Test. My parents were all enthusiastic, my teachers loved me. That was going to be my specialism, and then later my work assignment, and then my actual work. I had it all planned out. Then I passed the Test— failed it, more like—and it was all down the tubes.

"Not yet," I said. "I was going to at lunch, but I had to redo some work," bloody Comm Alren, "and this morning the brats were up early being annoying." The brats being my siblings. I'm the oldest. My and Kira's generation, there's not so many of us, because there were population restrictions. Alicante was launched twenty years ago, and about ten years ago, it was established enough that they relaxed the population restrictions a bit. Plus Gennaro was being planned, then.

So lots of us, like me, have a couple of sibs ten years or more younger. Kira's an only child, still. I am quite often envious. But now that Gennaro's sunk, everyone's kind of panicking a bit about space again and wondering whether we should have been more cautious. It makes it worse that Gennaro was only a quarter living space, and the rest for food and cloth and so on. I mean, we've never gone hungry in my lifetime, not properly *hungry*, but there were some bad times, before I was born, and everyone still worries about what happens if we have a bad season.

I bit my lip, and wondered if whoever was eating fish had anything to do with Gennaro. Did they resettle everyone, or were there people who, like, stayed out there, on their own ships or something maybe? How would they be eating?

"You OK, Jennery?" Kira asked, head slightly tilted.

"Yeah," I said. It wasn't my problem. Ocean would tell someone else, and they would sort it out. "I just haven't played today; you know it makes me cranky." I would make a shitty Communicator. It was best if I just kept quiet and waited for someone else to fix it.

Kira beamed at me. "So, how about now? Play me something, Jennery!"

I couldn't help but smile. My parents, these days, they still like to hear me, but they don't really understand. No one at the Centre cares, and I'd hate them to know anyway—if I play at lunchtime, I find somewhere where no one's going to see or hear me. Kira's the only one who still asks me to play.

So I pulled my flute out of my bag, and ran up and down a couple of scales while I waited to decide what to play. As ever, just feeling my fingers over the holes, the tiny vibration of the smooth bamboo under my hands, soothed me. *This* is what I should be doing. The Communicators could get lost. There were more proto-Communicators than ever before now, anyway. It wasn't like back at First Contact where Communicators were nearly non-existent. There were plenty now, and the insistence that if you *could*, you *must* was clearly way out of date. They didn't need me. Ocean didn't need me.

With Kira next to me, I remembered sitting on the floor when we were little, singing the rhymes and kids' songs they wrote on the ships, that my sibs are learning now. I started playing one of them.

"It all goes around, it all comes around," Kira joined in, half-smiling as xe leant just slightly against me.

There were stories they taught us along with the song, about the mistakes humans made on Old Earth, stories to scare and warn you. Though I'd learnt in the Centre that, if anything, the kids' versions were cut down, made less terrifying. The reality had been so much worse; it was almost hard to believe what Comm Alren told us. We were doing so much better here, making sure we didn't do any damage to the planet, or to Ocean. Even if it was hard sometimes.

Alongside that, though, as I played, I found myself wondering why the songs were still the same ones my grandparents and great-grandparents had learnt on the ships. We still sing traditional Old Earth songs, too. Shouldn't we be writing our own songs, about here, about Ocean? There's a couple, sure, about First Contact, with a lot of emphasis on the importance of the Contract, but written in Old Earth styles. Nothing *newer*. If we're here, now, shouldn't our art and our history and our music reflect that?

Maybe I should tackle it once I was free. That was something important I could do. Only two more days. Ocean was big. Ocean had lots of Communicators to talk to. Ocean could take care of Ocean-self.

I WASN'T EXPECTING THE MESSAGE

to have reached anyone else by the next morning. After all, Ocean couldn't have realised straight away that I hadn't passed it on. But the real Communicators, the grown-up ones, talk to Ocean off and on all day, and always first thing in the morning, so I figured, when Ocean didn't hear reassurance that we were dealing with the situation, Ocean would tell someone else.

I was watching, all morning, for some kind of reaction, some sense that the Centre was preparing to send people out, whatever. Nothing. I got told off a couple of times for not concentrating in class, but by now that was pretty much what they expected of me. And everyone—me, the teachers, the others in my class—knew that I'd never heard a thing from Ocean and that tomorrow would be my last day.

Comm Alren was talking about First Contact again, and the way we found to live *with* Ocean, without screwing over (xe didn't use that phrase) another sentient species. If Ocean can be a species when there's only one Ocean. Sure, it includes lots of other species which aren't sentient on their own, but Ocean is singular. Singular containing multitudes, I guess. Was Ocean pleased, when we came, to have another sentience to talk to? Or resentful of our interruption of Ocean's solitude? I mean, once we'd got past the bit where Ocean was pissed off that we were stealing chunks of Ocean away.

"That's when Communicators took on the responsibility of continuing that arrangement, and of defending and enforcing the Contract," Comm Alren said, all solemn, and everyone nodded.

Yeah, right. Whatever.

Before lunch we all lined up for our daily dose of the waters.

As a kid, you learn: stay away from the water. Don't swim in it, don't splash it on yourself, if something falls in and you fish it out, use an implement not your hands, and decontaminate whatever it is afterwards to remove any Ocean-traces (and return any residue to Ocean). Drinking water and plant-growing water is all distilled in the treatment plants. There's a tiny swimming pool in Endeavour that they teach everyone to swim in (because if you do fall in you have to be able to stay afloat so you can be fished out and decontaminated), and a few weird people keep going there after that for fun. There's races, once a year. Apparently Alicante is thinking about building a pool too, so we can have inter-city races, but I'm guessing after what happened to Gennaro that might be a bit further off. Too much of a waste of space, now we're suddenly short all those farm-rafts.

So we're all taught to avoid Ocean-water at all costs, and then you turn twelve and there's the Test, where they make you drink a full beaker of the stuff. The Ocean. Then they wait to see if you throw up or not. I didn't. Surprise! Congratulations Jennery, you're off to be a Communicator.

No one knows why some people can drink it and some can't. Back before the Contract, they thought no one could, and our drinking water is still treated the same way as it was back then. After the Contract, it became clear that some people could (just one person, right at first). I guess scientists would have wanted to look into it, but Endeavour was pretty low on resources right around then, partly because of what Ocean did and partly because we had to stop eating fish, and investigating that wasn't a priority. By the time it was possible to put resources into it again, the Communicators had decided that the Contract meant not interfering with Ocean at all, and that covered any scientific investigation. My parent, Delas, has been trying for years to find a compromise so xe and xyr team can look at what's going on, especially now it seems more people are becoming Communicators, but xe hasn't had any luck yet.

In any case, the deal is, our scientists don't really know why, and all I know is that it's never been a priority for anyone. Those who can drink it, if they drink it regularly, can talk to Ocean. Delas thinks maybe there's some kind of microorganism that sets up shop in your body and somehow mediates the connection with

Ocean, though xe doesn't know how no one would have spotted it before; that's what xe wants to investigate, if the Communicators ever let xem. If the water doesn't make you sick, then whatever happens doesn't seem to affect health or longevity or anything like that. It just allows you to talk to Ocean. (Unless you're me. Well, unless you're me before yesterday.)

Regular drinking water doesn't taste of anything much. Water from Ocean tastes of all sorts of things. Apparently back on Earth, sea water was salty. Ocean isn't salty. It tastes slightly metallic, a strange flat feeling on the back of your tongue. But there's a sweetness to it, as well. I really *want* to hate it, because of everything it means, but I can't, even when I try hard. Drinking it makes my mouth tingle, and although the waters are cool, it feels warming as I swallow. I'll miss it when I leave.

One more day.

But before that there was another Communication session to get through. I put it off as long as possible, changing really slowly out of my dry clothes and into swimming stuff. I don't like seeing myself in swimming stuff. My skin's dark enough that if I'm covered up, if you can only see my face and hands, you don't always spot the silver glints that come from drinking Ocean water. Paler folk, like Comm Alren or Comm Tereth, they look silver all over. Partly that's time, but even the paler people who Tested in along with me look pretty silvery too. It's one of the ways people know you're a Communicator, so they can be weird around you. Helpful, right?

So I wear long sleeves a lot. But when I wear swimming kit, there's more skin visible and the silver shows up more. I hate it. The worst of it is, I don't even know if it's going to go away when I leave, when I can stop drinking the damn water. No one's ever Tested and not become a Communicator. There's provision for it, in the rules, but it's never happened. So when I'm done, the day after tomorrow, Comm Theo, who does medical care for us, said I'd just have to stop drinking it and we'll keep a close eye on what happens. Xe had a look that made me think xe was kind of looking forward to finding out.

So I was trying not to look at myself when I put my swimming kit on. And I was dawdling even more than usual, because—what if Ocean spoke to me again? What if Ocean wouldn't listen to me telling Ocean to talk to someone else? Except surely Ocean had spoken to someone else already. Surely Ocean would realise that I was no good, that it was best to leave me alone.

Comm Alren was supervising today.

"Come on, Jennery," xe said, irritably. "I know you can't wait to leave here, but there are two more days, and two more swims, and I'll thank you to get a move on and be done with it." Comm Alren rolled xyr eyes slightly. "If you don't log enough time today, I'll be forced to report that you haven't done enough overall and you'll be here for another day. Or more."

"All right, all right, I'm going," I said, and stomped past xem out to the cove where we go to swim.

The Centre is on a little peninsula, jutting out from the main body of Endeavour. It's attached to the mainland by a fairly narrow path, and then the buildings are built on a kind of crescent surrounding the cove. It's all part of the old ship, but I can't remember what Comm Alren said this bit was made from, or rather, I chose not to bother remembering. It's some weird Old Earth stuff that doesn't corrode, like all the other old bits, and it floats on the water like everything else. The buildings of the Centre are highest in the middle and get lower towards the edge and the changing rooms are right out on one end of the crescent, just a single-storey-height bamboo block. The older buildings are scavenged and hacked together from Endeavour, but the changing blocks are modern. The dock itself is smooth and shiny and the edge curves so you can slide straight into the water and swim in the nearly-circle formed where the crescent curves inwards at each end.

Everyone else was out there already, floating on their backs or diving under the surface or swimming out and back, whatever suited them best. No one was looking for me. I never made any secret of the fact that I didn't want to be here, which was possibly a tactical error. You'd think that after nearly four years we'd have come to some kind of détente, but apparently not. Screw them all. A day and a half left.

I jumped in and floated on my back. Using as little energy as possible has always been my main goal in these sessions. And getting through them without Ocean speaking to me. Ocean's water is just about the perfect temperature for humans. It's just a little cool when you first get in, but warm enough that you get accustomed to it almost immediately and it stays comfortable pretty much indefinitely. Ocean water feels soft against your skin; soft and reassuring. I might not want to be a Communicator, but floating quietly alone in Ocean feels amazing.

Ocean is kind of amazing. I can admit that. I just don't want to *talk* to Ocean. I imagine a wall all around me, shutting Ocean out, and hoped like hell that it would work. Nothing to see here. Go away. Leave me alone.

I lay there, counting down minutes, and occasionally flipping over onto my stomach to stare down at the little fish swimming a few feet under me in the clear green water. Fish who trailed their tentacles behind them; fish with hundreds of tiny fins all over their bodies; fish with mighty propeller tails that corkscrewed through the water. (People were eating fish. I tried not to think about it.)

Maybe once I escaped being a Communicator, I could go looking for more fish, out in other parts of Ocean, places where no one would know or care that I was nearly a Communicator. Maybe Kira would come with me, and I could swim and look for fish and Kira wouldn't care that I was a bit silvery and I'd play the flute for both of us in the evenings.

The bubbles started up again, and my stomach sank, my lunch feeling heavy and indigestible inside me. So much for my mental wall. The bubbles were more insistent this time, and a little puzzled. I found myself trying to explain, in my head, why I hadn't told anyone. The puzzlement didn't go away. I don't think Ocean is equipped to understand that sort of human motivation. Ocean told me more, this time, about where it was, and how it was still happening, had happened again, and we had to *do* something. Ocean was distressed, as far as I could tell, and Ocean distressed is likely to strike out.

That was one of Comm Alren's lessons I did remember, something that we all learnt in baby school too, about what happened before the Communicators, before we made the Contract.

One more day.

I told Ocean, over and over again, to tell *someone else*. And then I got out and told Comm Alren that no, I still hadn't heard anything, and I hoped as hard as I could that it would all be OK in the morning.

I HAD MY WORK ASSIGNMENT that afternoon after the Centre. Most things have people who specialise in them, but there's a bunch of tedious tasks that everyone has to put the time in to get done. Today I was down for work in the flax fields, which is pretty much my favourite assignment. (My least favourite, like everyone else, is dealing with sewage at the pre-compost stage.)

I find the whole process of harvesting and preparing flax soothing. Today someone else was already checking the drying bundles, and there weren't any plants ready for pulling, but the water in the retting tanks needed to be changed. After that, I broke up some dry retted stuff, getting the outsides off to go to the compost collector, and the insides ready to pass to someone for heckling. I don't have the dexterity for spinning, even if I hadn't been sent off to be a Communicator and anyway, I wanted to do music, but I like knowing that when I get a new shirt, I probably handled the plants it came from, somewhere along the line.

After I was done with the flax, I went to the dock, but Kira didn't show. I guessed xe was working with Stel. Which meant that I had nothing to distract me from the question that kept coming up in my head—what if Ocean didn't tell anyone else? What if Ocean didn't, and I didn't? Ocean ignored could be dangerous, everyone knew that. We all knew what happened before First Contact, when Ocean was trying to get our attention and couldn't. Ocean isn't human. Ocean didn't understand what it was doing. Ocean still isn't human. What might Ocean do this time? I thought again about that sunken island. Ocean might not have done that, but what if... I saw an imagined Gennaro in my mind's eye, bamboo scattered, floating bodies, desperate people in tiny boats... and then I saw Endeavour, fractured the same way, Kira's body face-up in the water, Ocean's waves lashing the city.

I didn't sleep well. I woke up sandy-eyed and went down to breakfast.

Delas was at the stove, cooking pancakes, my favourite treat, and not something xe usually had time to make in the mornings. Reth was at the table with the brats, but xe jumped up and came to give me a hug.

"Happy birthday, Jennery!"

Delas turned round, handed me a plate with two rolled up pancakes, and gave me a kiss on the cheek.

"Thanks," I said gruffly, and sat down. There was a little package at my place at the table, and once I'd eaten the first bite of pancake—there was sweet jam inside, another rare treat—I unwrapped it. It was a gold shirt, my favourite colour, but one they only occasionally grow dye plants for. I swallowed hard, and got up to give Reth and Delas another hug apiece.

"You must have been saving yarn for ages," I said, and Reth nodded.

"Sixteen though," xe said. "It's a big day for my baby." Xe nudged me with xyr shoulder.

"I'm not a *baby*," I said, rolling my eyes.

"You'll always be my baby," Reth said cheerfully, and I couldn't help but laugh.

"You're not going to be a Communicator, are you?" Terren, my six-year-old sibling, demanded, and just like that, my cheerful mood evaporated. "I thought *everyone* in the Centre gets to be a Communicator. You're weird."

Surely Ocean would have told someone by now. Surely.

"No," I said. "I'm not."

Reth bit xyr lip. My parents always knew I didn't want this, but from where they stand, it's an honour and a privilege to be a Communicator.

"I want to be a Communicator," Terren said. "You're stupid, not wanting to."

"Good for you," I said, through gritted teeth. "Maybe you will be. Whatever." I turned to my parents. "So that means I can start musician training tomorrow, right?"

Delas pulled a face. "Maybe you should take just a little time after you leave the Centre…" xe said.

"You'll need to find someone to take you on," Reth added.

I'd held it against them for ages after the Test, that they'd made me go to the Centre, that they hadn't found me a way out of it. I'd gotten over that—mostly—but it hurt like hell that they *still* weren't properly supportive, even now I would be out of the Centre.

"What, do you think that's going to be a problem?" I demanded. "I'd have found someone already if you'd just let me get it set up." They'd said I couldn't find a mentor until I was actually out of the Centre. And maybe they were right and no one would have agreed for certain before that, but I still hated that they'd forbidden me from even *asking*.

"It's not that we doubt you," Delas said, obviously intending to sound calming. Xyr tone just annoyed me more. "We've never doubted you, love. It's just, this has all been a big deal, and maybe it makes sense to spend a bit of time thinking about your next steps before jumping into anything."

"Just because you wanted me to be a Communicator," I said. "I never did. You know I didn't. I've been *thinking about* this for four sodding years."

"Sodding years!" Hylla, my four-year-old sibling, echoed happily, and Reth frowned at me.

"Oh hell, I'm going to be late," Delas said, hastily swallowing the rest of xyr tea.

"Hell!" Hylla said, and Reth frowned at Delas instead.

Xe didn't notice. "We've got a meeting with the Communicators later."

"Still trying to get that Ocean project authorised?" Reth asked, and Delas nodded. Xe'd been trying that for ages. The Communicators had always been reluctant, and then there was the resource issue… I couldn't see that any of it was about to get any easier, not with the whole Gennaro situation.

"That's why you're annoyed that I'm not going to be a Communicator, isn't it?" I said, nastily. "Now you can't get me to intervene for you."

"Oh Jennery, love, I'm not annoyed, of course not. I know you never wanted this. We just want you to be happy…" Delas' face crumpled.

"Then you could have got me out of this before now," I snapped, unfairly, and banged out of the door, abandoning my new shirt on the table.

I FELT GUILTY ALMOST AS soon as I'd left, but that feeling was subsumed under a cold layer of dread about whether or not Ocean had spoken to anyone else. I told myself, all the way to the Centre, my feet dragging, that it would be fine. But it wasn't. There was no sign of anyone being anxious, no bustle of Communicators preparing to go off and investigate something. I even asked Comm Alren if there was any trouble right now, and xe said no, and gave me a strange look, and said something about concentrating in class even if it was my last day.

I didn't concentrate at all. I sat there and stared out of the window, chewing at my nails.

Ocean was upset. Ocean hadn't told anyone else.

We have a responsibility, Comm Alren said in my head, even as real out-loud Comm Alren said something I wasn't paying any attention to.

But why did it have to be *my* responsibility? I was nearly out. I was so, so nearly out. I could go and do what I wanted to. It wasn't like being a musician wasn't a perfectly reasonable social goal, and I was good enough, I knew I was. Or I would be once I was practising properly again. I had all these plans, to start writing things that really reflected our lives here. Wasn't that a responsibility, too? Ocean had plenty of people to talk to. Why couldn't Ocean just use one of them.

But Ocean hadn't. Ocean had spoken to me. For whatever bizarre reason, Ocean had spoken to me and to no one else. If I didn't do something about this, then no one else could, because no one else knew. Which meant that whatever happened next would be my fault.

I saw, again, those floating bodies. We have a responsibility. *Fuck.*

So I went to Comm Tereth, and I told xem, and I listened inside my head to the sound of the gates clanging shut. Happy birthday to me.

COMM TERETH GAVE ME A big smile once
I was done talking. "Of course this is serious news, but aside from that, it is wonderful to be able to welcome you as one of us, Jennery. I remember the first time I spoke with Ocean—it was a little scary, initially, yes, but since then I've had the joy of being able to communicate with a wholly different sentience! I know that every Communicator develops xyr own relationship with Ocean, and I hope that you enjoy developing your relationship over time." Xyr face was painfully sincere.

I didn't *want* a relationship with Ocean. I didn't want to get to know Ocean. I had people in my life already. Like Kira. Kira who thought Communicators were weird. I pushed the thought away.

Comm Tereth seemed to be waiting for a response. Xyr smile dimmed a little when I didn't say anything.

"Well," xe said. "This is a big day for you, so I think it's fine for you to miss the rest of the day, go home, and tell your family. We will investigate your report, and see if other Communicators can get a little more out of Ocean." A tiny frown appeared on xyr face. "I could wish you'd told us immediately, Jennery, but I suppose… I can understand that it was a surprise. We'll talk about next steps tomorrow, yes? First thing tomorrow."

Xe nodded, dismissing me, and I got out of there as fast as I could. I didn't get my stuff from my locker. I didn't want to talk to anyone else. I went straight out of the gates and home.

My parents were both home for lunch. They were visibly torn between pride—their child a Communicator, finally—and sympathy, knowing that I hadn't wanted this even if they'd never really understood why.

"You can still play for yourself," Reth said at one point, trying to reassure me, and I forced a smile and nodded.

I thought of going to find Kira, but then I remembered what xe had said two days before. Something in my gut twisted and I couldn't bear to. So instead I just went to my room and contemplated the rest of my life, stretching out ahead of me with no music in it, just whatever the Communicators did all day. I didn't even really know what that was. I'd pinned all my hopes on *escaping* this stupid business.

I trudged back in the next morning without looking at anything around me. I'd thought, briefly, in the middle of the night, about running away, but where and how would I run? It's not like it's like Old Earth here, where there was food everywhere for the picking and space, so much space. Here, its water all around, water you can't even drink (though, hah, I guess I can), and you need ships and platforms to live on and to grow things and it's just not possible to go out on your own. There are a handful of hermits, out on the far seas, but even they rely on coming into villages every so often for food and major boat maintenance stuff.

And when it came down to it, part of me said: *you've made your decision. Now stick with it, and may it choke you.*

I really did have to tell Kira, though. I felt bad today, thinking that xe would have missed me yesterday afternoon, maybe waited for me, and I hadn't so much as sent word. This afternoon, once I was done here, I would go find xem, and confess. Kira had always been on my side. Xe would understand, in the end. Surely?

There was a message on my locker when I got in, to go see Comm Tereth immediately. Well. Whatever. I trudged off to the office, instead of to lessons. Although presumably I was done with lessons, now, too? I really hadn't paid any attention to what would happen next if I didn't get out. I'd been going to *get out.*

"Well," Comm Tereth said when I showed up. "As you are aware, this incident you reported is high importance, and we've put a team together to investigate it. You're to be part of it, Jennery, as the person Ocean first reported to." Xe stopped, and tilted xyr head. "We'll induct you as Comm Jennery when you get back, yes? This is more important, I'm afraid."

I barely refrained from rolling my eyes. I didn't *want* the stupid title, surely xe knew that. I was hardly likely to mind whether I got it tomorrow or next month or, hey, how about never.

I wasn't mad keen on shipping out to the middle of nowhere to chase down illegal fishing, mind, either.

"This is part of the job, now that you are one of us," Comm Tereth was still going on. "Comm Alren will be going with you, as senior Communicator, and you'll take a couple of mechanics since this seems to be linked to the failure of Gennaro. Law enforcement will also be accompanying you."

"Comm Alren?" I said before I could stop myself. I was fairly sure the horror in my tone was noticeable.

"Alren is an experienced Communicator, and has dealt with similar situations before," Comm Tereth said. "I'm sure you'll both do just fine." Xe beamed at me. I was fairly certain xe wasn't faking it.

Crap. I'd definitely have to catch up with Kira this afternoon, then, before I left.

Comm Tereth was still talking. "You'll be leaving this afternoon. Go home and pack a bag, and be back here for lunch."

Well, shit.

AS I PACKED THE BAG and explained to Reth, who was working at home that day, where I was off to, I gave serious consideration to the whole hermitting business. Maybe it could be done after all. It seemed a damn sight of a better idea than spending who knows how long (how would we even find these people, in the middle of planet-sized Ocean?) on a boat with Comm Alren and whoever else I was being shipped off with. I had to make do with leaving a note for Kira, who was at work.

"I hear you're finally a Communicator now, Jennery?" xyr parent said when I stopped by to deliver the note.

Great, so Kira would have heard already, and not from me. I muttered something about being late, and escaped.

When I got back, my bag over my shoulder, Comm Alren was standing by the door to the lunch hall.

"Ah, good, Jennery."

"Comm Alren," I greeted xem, politely.

Xe waved an impatient hand. "Alren will do fine. You're not a child any more, Jennery. You're one of us, now." For the first time ever, xyr gaze was almost approving. I tried not to feel unnerved. "Now, the rest of the team are already in Tereth's study. Come along."

Xe set off along the corridor without looking round to see if I was following.

I trailed reluctantly after xem.

Comm Tereth's study was crowded when we reached it, with a good dozen folk milling around talking at one another. I wondered, again, if they'd miss me if I made a run for it. Then someone said "Jennery!" and I turned around.

"Kira?" I said, sounding like an idiot.

"Isn't it exciting?" xe said. "They want Stel to go and look at where Gennaro sank, and Stel said I could come too! And then we got here and your boss said you would be coming with us!" Presumably "my boss" was Comm Tereth, although the label didn't quite feel appropriate. Kira frowned at me. "Although, Jennery, why on earth didn't you tell me?"

"Tell you what?" I asked.

"That you'd heard something!" Kira looked suddenly awkward, and xyr voice dropped, "Look, I know, well, you know. That you weren't… But it is exciting, isn't it, Jennery? And surely you knew I'd want to know!"

There was something slightly artificial about xyr performance of delight. The way Kira's eyes kept sliding off mine.

"It only happened yesterday," I said, which was the lie I was sticking to with everyone else, after all. "And it was late by the time I got out, and, well…"

"Yes, I'm so sorry I wasn't there yesterday," Kira said. "Stel got word late of the expedition, and we had so much stuff to get ready."

I hadn't been there either. But I felt, irrationally, hurt. Kira'd missed the day before, too. I waved a hand and muttered that it didn't matter. It didn't. It wasn't fair for me to expect Kira always to be there, except that xe always *had* been, before.

"Isn't it exciting, though?" Kira said again, smiling but not really smiling.

About as exciting as a tooth extraction, if you asked me, but I couldn't see myself explaining that here. Although—Kira *knew*. Xe *knew* I hadn't wanted this. Why was xe pretending? Well, I was pretending to have forgotten that Kira had told me Communicators were weird. There was that. Maybe we both had reason to pretend. Maybe if we pretended hard enough, it would all just blow over.

Comm Alren appeared in front of me, towing someone in law enforcement uniform.

"Jennery, good. This is Serah."

Serah was tall, and broad, and unsmiling. In that respect at least, xe looked a lot like Comm Alren. Xyr dark hair was shaved close to xyr scalp.

"This is Jennery, who was told about the problem by Ocean," Comm Alren explained.

"Good," Serah said. "I want as much information as I can before we set off. I need to know what we will have to take with us and what we're getting into."

"Um," I said, intelligently. "I haven't really yet… That is, Ocean hasn't…"

"What Jennery is trying to say is that xe is due to go and speak more with Ocean today," Comm Alren interrupted smoothly, which was just as well, as Serah's frown had been deepening with every word I spoke.

"Hm," Serah said. "Well. You must do that immediately after this meeting. I need a direction. I need to know what *numbers* we are talking about. I have to pull my people away from their normal jobs to deal with this, and we do not wish to be more short-handed here on Endeavour than is absolutely necessary." Xyr voice was harsh.

"Jennery will speak with Ocean when the time is right to do so," Comm Alren said with a thread of steel in xyr own voice. "And then xe will pass on the information you need to know."

Comm Tereth called us all to order, and the conversation ended. But Serah's attitude didn't exactly fill me with enthusiastic optimism about this little trip.

IT TOOK US THE REST of the day to get underway. Ocean didn't seem to really understand my questions, as relayed from Serah, about numbers or directions. Ocean, I was pretty sure, just didn't think in those terms. Or, since all I could do was to interpret Ocean through my own experience, maybe I wasn't thinking in Ocean's terms. I had a headache by the time I gave up and got out of the water. The best I'd been able to do was to place the fishers near the current that Gennaro had set out into, which wasn't much more than we could have guessed for ourselves. Serah was visibly frustrated with the fact that I couldn't give xem exact co-ordinates and, I dunno, a full detailed description of every boat, adult, and child out there, despite the fact that Comm Alren kept stepping in—to my surprise—to defend me.

"Ocean simply does not engage in this kind of bean-counting," xe declared. "You know that well enough. We must work with what we have."

Serah and Comm Alren sniped about it all afternoon, antagonism thinly disguised in claims by both that they simply wished to set the expedition off on the best footing. Comm Alren suggested that a comparison between Gennaro's original membership list and the returning refugees might provide the numbers Serah was so desperate for. Serah pointed out that the Gennaro refugees were quite clear that there had been drownings, and no one seemed to know anything about missing-but-not-drowned Gennarans. Then wondered aloud why there had been no Comms sent with Gennaro. I wondered that too. I also wondered why no one was talking about the drowned bodies. Didn't they breach the Contract, by going into Ocean instead of being processed by us? Why wasn't Ocean kicking up about them? But then there were also the drownings before the Contract, before First Contact… I noticed I'd chewed my lip to bleeding, and gave up. Not my affair.

I didn't want to be here. I'd never wanted to be here. I'd done my bit by reporting what I'd heard, wholly screwing myself over in the process. Serah and Comm Alren would deal with it all now, and good luck to them.

THE NEXT MORNING, WELL OUT of sight now of Endeavour, I sat under the lee rail with my feet dangling over the edge. I'd taken my new gold shirt with me, which at least made Reth happy even as xe was fussing about me going off at all, and I was wearing it. The shirt made me happy, too, truth be told, even if it didn't even begin to balance out everything else.

It was a calm day, and easy sailing, the wind nicely in our favour. A little further along the deck, Kira was talking to Stel. Stel's dark braids were wrapped away from xyr dark brown face in a red scarf. It was warm enough today for xe not to wear an undershirt with xyr faded blue overalls, and xyr muscled arms and shoulders indicated the physical side of xyr job. I'd watched Kira get visibly stronger during xyr apprenticeship, too. Stel's pockets were weighed down with what I assumed were the tools of xyr trade, and a highly polished metal spanner and hammer were tucked into xyr belt. Kira, nodding earnestly at whatever Stel was saying, wore a similar belt over xyr own overalls, but no sign of any tools. Metal was far too precious for apprentices to cart around with them.

Stel grinned suddenly at Kira, and made a shooing gesture, before turning away xemself to walk towards the stern. Kira turned, saw me, and came along the deck towards me.

"Stel says there's nothing much for us to be doing, so I might as well take some time off," xe said cheerfully. "Can I come sit with you?"

"Sure," I said.

Kira sat down next to me, xyr leg resting against mine. I wondered, a bit, whether I could get away with putting my arm around xem. We used to sit like that a lot, when we were kids.

"Do you know," I said, gazing down at the water, "that on Old Earth, boats used to be combustion-driven? No wonder it got in such a mess."

"Yeah?" Kira said, not that interested. "I like sailing. I like the feel of the wind."

"Mm." I stared down at the water under my feet. "You know, I can't help thinking—why are we having to do this at all?"

Kira frowned. "What do you mean? We're here because Ocean told you about illegal fishing. I guess that has to be fixed, right?"

"Yes, sure," I agreed. "Ocean was very unhappy. I guess I'd be unhappy if someone was chopping off parts of me. But that's not what I meant. *Why* are they doing it? I mean, would *you* fish?"

"Of course not!" Kira said, looking a bit repulsed.

"Right. So whoever this is, why are *they* doing it?"

"I suppose they must be hungry. Once the island sank, I mean."

"But they could have come back. Like the rest of the refugees from Gennaro. Which we all thought was everyone, right? So why didn't they? Why did they choose to do something like that to Ocean, instead?"

Kira stared out across the water for a while without saying anything, kicking xyr feet against the hull.

"I wonder sometimes," xe said, slowly, "if we're doing the right thing with all the Ocean business."

I frowned. "What do you mean?"

"Leo said," xe hesitated. Leo was that kid from Gennaro that Kira had the crush on, I remembered.

"Leo said that Ocean isn't sentient at all really and it's all just a lie."

"What?" I said indignantly, genuinely taken aback. "Of course Ocean is sentient! How can you say such a thing?"

"I didn't say I believed it, Jennery," Kira sounded sulky, and not entirely convincing. "I said that's what

Leo said. That it's all just about the Communicators wanting to control everyone else." Xe looked at me. "You ought to know about that, right?"

I hated the way that sounded; that I was a Communicator now. I mean, okay, I was a Communicator. But I didn't want Kira to think of me that way.

"Well, none of my classes were, like, Mind Control For Beginners, if that's what you mean," I said, going for light-hearted and missing by half a klick. "But anyway, that's just nonsense. I've *heard* Ocean, remember? Myself. Ocean is there, and Ocean thinks."

Kira was still looking out to sea, away from me. "I did wonder a bit. When you were there for so long, and never heard anything. I wondered if maybe people were just convincing themselves they heard something. Or saying that they were."

"I didn't *want* to hear anything," I pointed out. "I did my level best to convince myself I *hadn't* heard anything." I remembered I didn't want to tell anyone, not even Kira, that part, and shut my mouth again. It didn't matter, after all. Here we were anyway.

"I know. But you spent a lot of time there. Everyone kept telling you you ought to be hearing stuff. Maybe…"

I was getting really pissed off. "That's crap, Kira. I didn't talk myself into something I didn't want. You *know* how I felt about this."

"But you *are* one of them now," Kira said, and it felt like a punch in my stomach. "So, I mean… Look, Ocean has such strict rules. Here we are, heading off across the sea to a place where a whole bunch of people drowned, and Ocean… And we don't know why."

"And Ocean what?" I asked, but xe was still talking.

"A load of people actually died, and a lot more nearly died of hunger before they could get back. And Ocean is freaking out about some fish. And Leo told us about being out there, trying to get back, and they stuck to the rules, they didn't eat the fish, and they nearly *died*. Why does Ocean get to call the shots like this?"

"Well, because Ocean was here first," I said. "We shouldn't be here at all, when it comes to it, right? I mean, if the survey had shown up the fact that Ocean was sentient, no one would have come here at all."

"Maybe they should have gone straight back again," Kira said.

"Oh come on, Kira. They couldn't. It wasn't even straight away that anyone realised. The ship was Endeavour, by then. No way home, and no chance that Old Earth would come and rescue them."

"Yeah, yeah, I know the story," Kira said. "Communicators, the Contract, blah blah. But that was *then*. This is *now*. Why do we have to stick by something over a hundred years old? We live here too, now, it's not just

Ocean's planet. Why are we tiptoeing around Ocean like this? When is it *our* turn? It's our planet too." Kira folded xyr arms defiantly.

"Because no one wants Ocean to get angry again like before First Contact?" I said. Though angry might not be quite right. Ocean didn't have emotions like a human did. Didn't stop it from being destructive.

"Then Ocean's holding us hostage," Kira said flatly. "Expansion is so *slow*. Everyone worries about food all the time. And then you look out at all that protein gallivanting around in the bay..." Xe stopped and grimaced. "Okay, I'm exaggerating, that's just too grim to think about. We're fine for food. But maybe if we could build on the coral that's just under the surface over to the west, rather than it having to be always islands, with that hard limit on how quickly we can grow bamboo... We're not working *with* Ocean, Jennery. We're *avoiding* Ocean. And the Comms are the only ones who can talk to Ocean, and you're not doing anything about any of it, just carrying on the same way for ever." Kira's voice was intense, and xe was speaking more loudly now.

"So just because you're, I don't know, *fed* up of how we do things, maybe Ocean's all just a lie made up by Communicators to control everyone, like Leo says?" I jeered. I felt sick, hearing Kira say all of this stuff. We had to protect Ocean. That had to be the most important thing. And how could Kira possibly think that Ocean wasn't sentient?

Kira folded xyr arms, glaring at me. "People wonder. People are *unhappy*, you know?"

"Do you believe that? That it's all just a lie?"

"That's not what I said. You're not *listening*, Jennery."

"You're accusing me of things!"

"You're a Communicator now, aren't you?" Kira challenged me, xyr eyes narrowing.

I hunched my shoulder. "I don't have an option, do I." I swallowed, trying to see past the hurt of Kira speaking like this to me. "Look…"

"Kira!" Stel shouted along the deck.

"I've got to go," Kira said, scrambling to xyr feet. Xe almost ran away from me along the deck.

I kicked my own heels against the hull, and swore under my breath for a while. Now even Kira didn't want to talk to me; even Kira thought I was one of *them* now.

I wanted to think that xe was just wrong, but I couldn't wholly dismiss it, even though I tried. The idea that the Contract was old, that the Comms were failing… It fit in with how Serah had been too. Our job was supposed to be mediating between Ocean and the rest of the humans, but it seemed like we weren't doing it very well, if people like Kira could be saying stuff like this.

I wondered if I should go and talk to Comm Alren. But xe couldn't *not* know this, couldn't have missed how Serah was being. The Centre must know what people were saying. They just hadn't told kids like me, not-yet-Communicators. And I'd been so busy sulking and ignoring everyone else for the last four years that I hadn't picked up on it without being explicitly told.

I'd just be told I was overreacting. Or that Kira was overreacting. The proper Communicators must have it all in hand.

I really, really wished that Ocean had just kept Ocean's damn mouth shut. I should have been out of all of this by now. It wasn't *fair*.

IT WAS ANOTHER TWO DAYS before we reached the area where Gennaro had come apart, and where we were expecting to find the fishers. It was a long way away. Gennaro had deliberately been taken out to a different current, one that never came all that close to Endeavour because of weather patterns and stuff, and as it happened, right now that particular spot in it was a long way away from Endeavour's place in its own current. For sure, we were out of radio range of Endeavour by now, which felt a bit weird.

Kira wasn't exactly not talking to me, but xe always seemed to be very busy doing things for Stel. At any rate, we weren't hanging out, and there was hardly anyone else on board I was likely to hang out with. (I could just see me and Comm Alren having a nice friendly chat. Oh no, wait, the other thing.) I badly wanted to get my flute out, but there was nowhere I could go on the boat where people wouldn't hear, and I couldn't bring myself to perform, even by accident. The thought hurt, like a sore tooth.

So I had plenty of time to think about what Kira had said. A little bit about how the Communicators were maybe getting out of touch. But mostly about the idea that the Contract might be out of date.

The Contract said that we didn't eat fish, or anything from Ocean, because they were all part of Ocean. It would be like Ocean eating someone's arm or leg. But then—wasn't that exactly what happened *within* Ocean? We didn't actually know all that much about Ocean's ecosystem, but we did know that big fish ate the little fish, and little fish ate littler fish and littler fish ate the algae and all the rest of it, all the way down and back round again. It was an ecosystem. Ocean had its own ecosystem, and the humans had our own ecosystem, resting precariously on top of Ocean's. Because none of our stuff went back into Ocean; that was part of the Contract, too. We composted our food leftovers and our waste, and used them to grow our food. We used distilled water to drink and wash and grow crops. We broke down human remains and put them back into the soil system. We avoided—other than Communicators—going into the water. There were in theory only two points of contact: the water that the Communicators drank and swam in and the bamboo that we used to extend rafts. That grew separately from all the other plants, separate even from the bamboo for building on top of the rafts, with its feet in Ocean, and it was only used for the rafts, where it would be in contact with Ocean's water. Endeavour was in contact too, but Endeavour was made from this non-rusting non-rotting Old Earth stuff. That had been part of the colonists' original plan: waste not want not.

So. Two points of contact, and, now I came to think of it, both bamboo, and to some extent Communicators, were separate from the rest of the human ecosystem too, which seemed kind of interesting.

But could we really keep things this way forever? Keeping separate from Ocean made perfect sense *if* you thought we would all be going back to Earth someday. Surely if we were here for good, we should find a way to join the systems up?

I was chewing this over when Comm Alren came to sit with me.

"So, Jennery. How are you adjusting to being a Communicator?" Xyr voice was surprisingly kind.

I hadn't meant to say anything about it, but I found myself asking, "Why do we stay so separate? People say—" I caught myself. I didn't want to get Kira into trouble, even if xe was avoiding me. "I mean, doesn't it make it harder for us to mediate, if none of us know any non-Communicators?"

Comm Alren gave me a patronising smile and talked for ages about *understanding* Ocean, and a bit about the perils of contamination, and none of it made any real sense at all.

"You are correct that it is important to talk to others, though," xe finished up. "Which reminds me, I see Serah over there…"

Xe got up and walked purposefully up the deck.

I wasn't convinced by anything xe had said. But the conversation didn't encourage me to ask about fish and the Contract.

Comm Alren had said one thing that made me think—xe had referred to overcrowding at the Centre. I'd already known that more people were able to be Communicators than there used to be. A generation before, it was one person a year, or none at all. There were four in my year, and three the year below, and the others had all spoken to Ocean pretty quickly. Communicators were the ones with some weird adaptation to Ocean. So did that mean that we, as a population, were changing, getting somehow closer to Ocean? We were all on the same planet. *Were* we as separate as we thought? *Did* that make the Contract out of date?

I badly wanted to talk to Kira about it, but no way was I going to go looking for xem right now.

But I couldn't let the idea alone. It niggled in the back of my head, all through those two days, all while I stared over the edge of the ship, into the water that sank away deep beneath us.

I kept coming back, too, to the question of what Ocean thought about the separation. It felt weird, wrong, even to ask the question. Ocean had demanded the Contract, and Ocean had told me about the fishing so we could enforce it. The Contract was sacrosanct, the most important thing in every decision. Everyone knew the horror story about when humans first met the Pyx, back before we left Old Earth. The Contract was what kept us from treating Ocean that way. And yet...

I could ask Ocean, I supposed. Now that Ocean had spoken to me. But I couldn't bring myself to hop into Ocean and ask. I couldn't think of a way to say it, even. And I'd have to get them to stop the ship, just for my whim, which gave me the shudders even to think about... and anyway, I wasn't *really* a Communicator, right? Not really. It wasn't right for me even to be thinking like this. I should leave it to the real Communicators; and they, I was sure, would tell me never to doubt the Contract. This wasn't any of my business.

At one point, while I was looking into Ocean, I saw one of those great fish humping its back over the surface of the water, and when I glanced along the ship, Serah was staring at it too. Here we were in our own ecosystem; with compost barrels at the bottom of the ship, storing our waste until we could return it to the big treatment plants on Endeavour. There was the great fish, in its Ocean ecosystem. Two systems, one planet. I looked at Serah and wondered if xe was thinking anything similar. Or maybe if, like Kira, xe was seeing it as a big lump of walking protein. Serah had to deal with the unrest when food was short. It must be in xyr mind. And there xe was down that end of the ship, and brand-new Communicator me up this end, and that was a problem too. But I could hardly even try to fix that either, barely-sixteen me telling my elders they were screwing up…

Serah looked up and saw me staring, narrowed xyr eyes, and stalked away from where xe had been leaning on the rail. I sighed, and watched the great fish disappear again, under the water and away.

WE GOT THERE ON THE morning of the third day, very early. I was still asleep, but a commotion brought me above deck, rubbing the sleep out of my eyes.

Kira was packing things onto one of the small boats, while Stel talked urgently to Comm Alren and Serah. Comm Alren was nodding in acceptance. Serah was scowling again.

"Yes, yes, we'll be in danger from a bunch of half-starved idiots," Stel growled at Serah, standing braced against the gentle motion of the ship. "Fine. I accept all of your warnings. But I'm not wasting valuable space on the boat with one of your lot. We have *work* to do."

"And *my* work is to keep everyone here safe," Serah said. Xe stood with xyr feet slightly apart, xyr arms folded.

I didn't understand why Serah was worried. Surely the survivors of Gennaro (if that was who these fishers were) would be in favour of Stel and Kira finding out what happened, so that we could build more islands in future, and perhaps they'd have somewhere to settle again. But then, they might not bother to distinguish between Stel and Kira fixing stuff, and me, Comm Alren, and Serah coming to stop them doing… whatever it was they were doing out here.

"I really must insist," Serah was saying. From the way xe said it, it wasn't the first time.

"It's all packed," Kira said, turning round.

Stel glanced into the boat, growled again to xemself, and turned back to Serah.

"Fine. *One* cop. And xe had better sit still, shut up, and do what I tell xem. If our work is disturbed…"

"I assure you, your work will be treated with all due respect," Serah said. Xe turned to the three law enforcement officers squatting on their haunches against the leeward rail, and gestured one of them up.

"Move everything around, Kira," Stel said. "Quick as you like. We need three seats now." Xe shot a look of dislike first at Serah, then at the cop who, to be fair, had jumped to help Kira repack.

No one was paying any attention to me. Not even Kira looked around for me before xe went. I watched as the boat was rearranged in double time, then lowered with Kira perched a little precariously among the boxes and packaged equipment. Xe looked both excited and nervous. Stel and the cop swung over the side of the ship, down a ladder, and dropped into the boat beside Kira, and then Stel hoisted the sail and they were off. They looked to be headed towards some floating fragments a little way away from us, which must be part of the remains of Gennaro.

I ought to go and find myself some breakfast, but I couldn't face moving from where I was slumped against the rope coils. Kira hadn't even *looked* for me. I told myself that xe was just busy—I wouldn't want to get against Stel either, however nice xe might be most of the time—and excited about the opportunity. I knew how important this was to xem. I should be supportive, and happy for xem, and stuff. But still. Xe hadn't even *looked*.

Eventually, I pushed myself onto my feet and slouched into the mess for coffee and flatbread. Comm Alren was already there, and nodded amiably enough at me. After a while I dared to ask xem what was happening.

"What is—I mean, what are we going to do, now we're here? About what Ocean said?" I asked.

"Serah will send out a couple of search boats," xe said. "I suppose they will find the miscreants, soon enough."

"Should I be doing something?"

Comm Alren shook xyr head. "Not until and unless Serah needs more information from you. Really, our main purpose here, you and I, is to serve as an indication that justice is in the process of being done. To observe the matter for Ocean, and to demonstrate to our own people our commitment to the Contract. And in your case, as a conduit of further information." Xe smiled at me. "Perhaps you should go for a swim, and let Ocean know that we are indeed acting on Ocean's information. Maintain the contact, that sort of thing."

"Right," I said, dully. "Sure." So there wasn't even a real reason for me being here at all.

"Do be careful to stay near the ship," xe added. "We don't know the currents around here terribly well, and we still don't know why Gennaro broke up. But you'll be safe enough close to the ship."

I didn't want to go into Ocean. I was fed up of Ocean. Ocean was why I was here; screw Ocean. But I couldn't face going back to my cabin either. For a while, I went back to the stack of rope coils, and watched Serah and the remaining cops going off in the other two small boats. One cop stayed behind to keep an eye on the useless folk (me and Comm Alren), and the ship's crew, busy at their jobs. Off in the distance, I could see the small figures of Kira and Stel in their boat, fishing this and that out of the water and poking at it. The blue of their protective gloves flashed as they worked.

Eventually even I got fed up with my own moping and decided to take up Comm Alren's suggestion. I would go for a swim. Do my duty, ugh, and talk to Ocean. It wasn't like there was anything else to do, and this was basically my job for the rest of my life now—go for a swim once a day, wait for Ocean to deign to communicate with me. Lucky me.

I waited until no one was wandering around on deck before I came back out of my cabin in my swimming kit. I still hated the faint tinge of silver on my skin. It didn't seem to show so much today; maybe the clouds were doing something funny to the light. I swung over the ship on the other side from where I could see Kira and Stel's boat—the idea of *Kira* seeing that silver bothered me even more—and struck out a little way away from it. Comm Alren had said to stay close, but a few metres was close enough. The ship wasn't going anywhere. I wanted to at least pretend that I had a little bit of distance. Though it was Ocean, really, that had trapped me; and there was no getting away from Ocean on this wretched planet.

I floated on my back, ears under the water. Despite my teeth-grinding frustration with, well, everything, I dutifully organised my thoughts so as to let Ocean know what was going on. At least then I could tell Comm Alren I'd done it. I didn't hear so much as a peep in return. Or a bubble. I stayed there for a while, sculling slightly with my hands, listening to the sound of the ship's hull underwater. It was peaceful, half under the water, nothing to be heard from Ocean, and the sun had broken through the clouds and felt warm on my face. I'd checked for currents, checked my position against the ship a few times, and there was nothing to worry about. I did my best not to think about anything at all—not even Kira—and I started to feel better. After a while, the sun went in, and I pulled myself upright to start swimming back to the ship.

It wasn't far. I could see that it wasn't far. And there hadn't been any currents, I'd *checked*. It should only be a few strokes back to the ship; but I was swimming and swimming and the ship wasn't getting any closer.

I was being pulled away.

I put more power into my swimming. I'm a strong swimmer.

It didn't help.

I looked around me. The water for a few feet in each direction was flowing differently from the water beyond that. This wasn't an accident, and—small reassurance—it wasn't my mistake. This was Ocean.

I called as loud as I could, then screamed, louder, until my throat hurt. But the wind blew in my face, and I knew, my heart sinking, that no one would hear me back on the ship. They'd miss me, eventually, but I was being pulled away faster and faster, and the ship was getting smaller and smaller...

I kept swimming, and I kept watching the ship recede into the distance. I could feel myself starting to get tired.

The ship vanished over the horizon, and I gave up and floated. I asked Ocean for help, first calmly, then angrily, shouting at Ocean in my mind. I realised after a while that I was shouting out loud. I got nothing back at all. Well, I hadn't wanted—didn't want—to be a Communicator. This was one way of avoiding it. Give up, stop floating, let Ocean drown me. Did Ocean know that would happen? Was Ocean deliberately killing me? Why? My throat was tight with pointless tears. I'd *done* what Ocean wanted, hadn't I?

After a while, I started to hear something. Something like a hull on water. Had they worked it out, after all? Had they come looking for me? I popped myself upright again and looked round. In the late afternoon light, there it was—a boat! A whole fleet of boats. Huh. Not my ship, then. Some travellers, maybe? Whoever it was, they would rescue me, surely they would rescue me. I waved, frantically, hands above my head, and heard shouts coming from one of the boats. It turned towards me, and for a moment I nearly let myself go under as I relaxed in relief. Then they were up to me, and people were pulling me out of the water. I collapsed on the deck, shivering violently.

"A *Communicator*?" I heard someone say. "Chuck xem back in."

"A *child*, or very nearly, and clearly unwell," someone else said. "Never mind who xe is, we've fished xem out and now we'll dry xem off and feed xem. You hear me?"

The first voice muttered something, but clearly the second voice was the one with the power.

"There now, child," the second voice said, propping me up to sitting and wrapping a blanket around me. "Onto your feet, now, and you just come with me, and we'll sort you out."

"Might be useful, at that," a third voice remarked, but I had no energy to worry about what xe meant right now. I was out of the water. I was alive. That was all I could think about.

THEY'D REALISED WHO I WAS

immediately. It took me a bit longer to figure out who they were. In my defense, the silver fucking skin is pretty obvious, and they hadn't just spent the previous half hour preparing to drown. I wasn't exactly entirely in my right mind for a few minutes.

The older person with the blanket introduced xemself as Bethany. Xe took me to a little cabin and shut the door behind us. It was very basic: two bunks bolted to the wall, two chests against the other wall with cushioned tops so you could sit on them, a couple of wall lights. Bare board floor with a rag rug pinned down. I'd noticed on the way to the cabin, despite my exhaustion, how small the boat was. It looked like a standard day-boat design: plenty of deck, two or three tiny cabins below, or one big one. But if this was a day-boat, pottering between rafts and islands, why did it have bunks in the cabin rather than seating? You didn't sleep on a day boat, not generally; you'd never be out that long. And what would it be doing all the way out here, anyway? I rubbed my forehead. I couldn't fit it together.

Bethany sat me down on the lower bunk. There was just about enough head height for me to sit up; it's handy being short, once in a while. Bethany fussed around, tucking the blanket around me like I was a little kid. Then xe stuck xyr head out of the cabin door and said something I couldn't catch to someone who was passing. I snuggled into the blanket and tried not to shiver. I was warming up, I told myself. I was fine. I was *dry* again, though I could really do with wearing some more clothes.

A few moments later, Bethany came back in again with a cup of soup. I drew the being-fussed-over line when xe attempted to feed it to me.

"I can manage for myself," I said, and took the spoon.

It was thin soup, mostly broth, with a few chunks of vegetables floating in it. The sort of thing I'd eaten a lot of growing up, every time the farms weren't doing so well. Bethany looked pretty skinny, now I came to look at xem, although xe was pretty old, too—xyr hair was grey, scraped back into a plait—and old people get that way.

Suddenly it all clanged into place. A flotilla of little boats, with not much food, out in the middle of nowhere, near where Gennaro had sunk, with people of all ages aboard.

"You're the fish people," I said.

Bethany just blinked at me, fake-innocent.

"Ocean told me," I said. Not much point in denying that I was a Communicator, after all. "Ocean said, there's people eating fish. Well, Ocean said the people were catching fish, so I'm guessing you were eating them, because otherwise why bother, right?" I struggled to keep the distaste out of my expression. This person actually *ate* fish.

"Is that so?" Bethany said.

I opened my mouth to say that there were a whole bunch of people looking for them now, then shut it again. Probably best not to give that away immediately.

"And you're here with, I presume, the police, looking for these Contract-breaking fishers?" Xe tutted at my ill-hidden look of surprise. "It's not like you can be here all on your own, child."

"I'm sixteen," I said sullenly. "I came out sailing with friends, for fun."

"No, you came with an enforcement team to find us," Bethany said. "We're not stupid, child. Although I can only suppose that *you* are, to wind up in the water all alone like that."

I couldn't work out if blaming Ocean would go down well or badly, so I just shrugged. Let xem think that. Whatever.

"So, what are you going to do with me?" I demanded.

"A good question," Bethany said. "Some would prefer to throw you straight back in again and let the ocean deal with you."

The ocean, I noticed. Not Ocean.

"I don't like that idea," I said. Just in case Bethany was wondering.

"I thought you Communicators loved to be in the water," Bethany said.

"We don't like drowning," I said. "Even Communicators can't just swim forever. And anyway, I never wanted to be a Communicator."

I wasn't sure if admitting that was a good or a bad idea, but it had the benefit of being true. Even if I did sound a bit like a sulky kid, saying it. And the way Bethany had been talking about Communicators, distancing myself from them a bit seemed wise.

I wondered what Comm Alren thought of my disappearance, and what xe and Serah were doing now about trying to find me. And then I wondered what Kira would think. I swallowed against a sudden lump in my throat, and put the soup spoon down.

"You should eat the rest," Bethany said. "You must have been out there a while. You will be tired."

I shook my head, miserably aware that if I said anything more I would burst into tears. Bethany's eyes narrowed, and xe leant forward again to look at me.

"You are tired," xe said, after a moment. "It's late. Rest here. I will speak to the others."

"What, so you can chuck me overboard while I'm sleeping?" I muttered.

Bethany sighed. "I give you my assurance, we will do nothing of the sort. Myself, I think there may be some use in your sudden appearance. At any rate, I am not in the business of drowning children. Or even sixteen-year-olds." Xe spoke with casual authority. Bethany certainly *believed* xe could keep me on board. What I wasn't sure about was whether xyr belief was correct.

I yawned hard enough that my jaw cracked. When it came right down to it, I couldn't stop them, if they did want to chuck me back over. Certainly not when I was this exhausted. Sleep might help. Couldn't hurt. I sighed, and lay down, pulling the blankets over me. It felt blissful. The lock on the door clicked shut behind Bethany as xe left. Even knowing that I was a prisoner didn't bother me enough to keep sleep away for any longer.

BETHANY WOKE ME UP THE next morning, with another bowl of that same soup, and hot water to drink.

Xe watched me as I ate, standing against the cabin door. Either the intentness of xyr gaze, or the soup and hot water, woke me up. I missed my usual morning infusion; presumably out here that was the sort of thing that was hard to come by. A luxury. It was odd, given how close to the bone everything often felt back at home, to think of us as having luxuries.

"So," I said, as I scraped out the bottom of the bowl. "What are you going to do with me, then?"

I felt a bit less nervous than I had last night. It seemed unlikely that they'd waste soup on me if they were going to throw me straight back over the side.

Bethany threw me a bundle of cloth.

"Put that on and come with me."

The bundle consisted of a slightly threadbare tunic and undertrousers, both a little too big for me.

Lacking much in the line of other ideas, I did as I was told, and followed Bethany out of the cabin.

It turned out that "come with me" meant "come and work with me". We went to the back of the boat, where they had vegetable trays stacked up against the stern rails, and a couple of layers above. Higher than you would normally have on a small boat like this, which can heel a lot in a storm; but the highest layers of trays were heavily braced; they were the ones that got more sunlight so were more valuable. Bethany told me to water them and add fertiliser. It was a small child's job, a job I did as a kid in the kitchen gardens around our neighbourhood on Endeavour.

Looking around, now it was daylight, I could see about a dozen other boats sailing near to us, all about the same size bar one that was a little larger. There were little kids at the back of some of them, and the side rails too, doing the same job I was; so it was whole families out here. Two or three cabins per boat, a family or a couple of adults per cabin... Somewhere between fifty and eighty people, maybe?

Next, the compost bins, tucked under the lower-most tray, had to be pulled out and turned over. It was soothing, somehow, doing the same jobs I used to do every day as a kid. But at the same time I was thinking: this isn't just for individual gardens. Out here they must be doing all their composting on this small, maximum-intervention scale, without any of the efficiencies I was used to on Endeavour.

Bethany took me to the side of the boat, and called to someone sitting on the deck over on the next boat across.

"Hoi! Gez! Coming over!"

Gez looked round, nodded, and threw the end of a coil of rope to Bethany, who secured it to a pulley in the rigging. Then Gez tipped a bosun's chair over the side and Bethany pulled it over. I'd seen them—I'd used one—for lowering off the side of a ship, but never for travelling between. Faster than a dinghy, though, fair enough, especially if this happened a lot.

"On you go, child," Bethany said.

I climbed over onto the chair and Gez hauled me over. It swayed more than I liked, but then, I didn't actually have to worry about falling in, not like everyone else here. Gez helped me up onto the deck, then sent the chair back for Bethany.

"This is the Communicator?" Gez said, and Bethany nodded. "Hm."

I didn't like the look that Gez gave me. Xe didn't say anything more, just shrugged and sat back down on the deck to go back to what xe had been doing—mending some kind of netting, it turned out.

Netting. Like, fish nets? I had in mind those old drawings of old Earth, and of the first few years when our ancestors first came to the planet. There was a fish net in the museum at the Centre. I swallowed.

It turned out that this boat housed a kitchen. I stiffened, looking around for fish, but all I could see were vegetables, and a paltry tiny lot of them, too. I was set to chopping, and Bethany warned me sharply not to waste any.

"We're not so well-provisioned at Endeavour we can afford to waste food," I said, slightly snippy, and Bethany raised an eyebrow before turning to xyr own task.

There was a sight more stock than there was vegetable in the soup they were making; the same broth I'd been given for the last two meals. And no grain, no pulses; no protein. Green leafy stuff, mostly, and that was all that had been in the vegetable trays I'd tended earlier, too.

"Do you not grow beans, or wheat?" I asked, after I'd been chopping for a while.

"A little," Bethany said. "But it grows badly in trays." As I knew. "We would need a proper raft, and for a proper raft you need bamboo, and we haven't enough."

And bamboo won't grow in trays, either.

"You could apply," I said.

"And we wouldn't get, unless we came in and attached ourselves back to Endeavour, or an island," Bethany said.

"What's so bad about that?" I asked. "You'd be supported. You'd have actual food in your hot water." I gestured at the big pans on the solar stove.

"We'd be there for good," Bethany said. Xe pushed a few strands of hair off xyr forehead, looking weary. "A year we had out here, a year of finally having some space, of being able to think of growing and spreading out, just a little. A year, and then the island fell apart, and what were our choices? Straight back to Endeavour where our old dwellings were already reallocated and we'd be back at the bottom of the housing list?" Xyr lips pressed tightly together as xe finished speaking, as if there were more that xe wasn't saying.

"Lots of people did just that," I said.

"Indeed so," Bethany said. "And that was their choice. And this is ours."

"But you can't survive like this," I said. "Without protein, without some kind of grain. It can't be done."

"Well now," Bethany said. "That depends, doesn't it?"

Lunch, it seemed, was eaten wherever you happened to be at the time. Bethany and I ate more of that vegetable soup, sitting in the back of the kitchen. The rest of it was decanted from the big pans into buckets with lids, then taken off to the surrounding boats by kids on the bosun's chairs.

"Now," Bethany said, after we'd finished. "I think this will be of interest to you."

I followed xem across three more chair-traverses and two more boat-decks. The boat we fetched up on was right on the edge of the fleet. There was a strong Ocean-like smell, not just Ocean surrounding us; more than that.

I gulped. Fishing. This was where they did the fishing. The people dotted around the boat were just starting their work again. What looked like tangled piles of rope or thick string lay around the deck, but as people picked them up and shook them out, two to each pile, they turned into—rope ladders, I thought for a moment, but no, cargo nets.

Not cargo nets. Fishing nets. Fishing nets, with weights tied to their edges. Two people to a net, they threw them overboard. Each person had a rope, and each pair lowered their weighted net further downwards. There were three nets, all lowered off the windward side. I watched in silence, Bethany next to me, from the leeward side of the deck.

I was torn. Part of me was horrified, revolted, by what I knew was about to happen. This was what Ocean had told me about. This was what I was supposed to be preventing. I was supposed to be out here catching these people and bringing them to justice, on behalf of Ocean. Surely I ought to do something—cut the ropes, or run forward shouting, or just denounce them, or *something*.

But part of me was deeply curious as to exactly what was happening. And I hadn't, actually, seen any wrongdoing, quite yet. Perhaps the nets were a pollutant, but that was fairly minor, and it would depend on what exactly they were made of. The fishers were handling the nets with gloves, so it might be that they were Ocean-compatible stuff themselves.

And part of me was still thinking about that idea I'd been chewing over back on the ship. Ocean had fish which ate other fish. Ocean had an eco-system. We had an eco-system. Was that separation right? Was this really as wrong as my back-brain was screaming at me that it was?

They pulled in a net.

For a moment, I thought I was going to be sick; a wave of nausea at the wrongness of the sight almost overwhelmed me. The net was half-full of fish, their bodies gleaming from the water pouring off them and back into Ocean. As the net came fully onto the deck, the water ran down onto the deck, then back off again and back into Ocean in channels carved into the deck. I looked down automatically at my feet, then realised that Bethany and I, and those working the nets, were all standing on planks raised just above the surface of the deck. These people were *eating* fish and yet they were still avoiding Ocean's water. How did that make any sense at all?

The fish were writhing, clearly still alive, gasping for the water they were no longer surrounded by. Their fins and tails and their long bodies flopped around, finding no resistance in the air that now surrounded them. I felt a deep inner pang, feeling inside myself that difference between moving through water and moving through air; but I was used to the difference, experienced it daily. And I wasn't going to die purely from being on either half of that divide.

My nausea had retreated a little, giving way instead to a desire to jump down from my little raised plank onto the deck, to take the net and thrust it back over the edge, return Ocean's fish to their home. To the rest of their self. That was the point, right? That was why we mustn't fish. The fish were part of Ocean. It was like if

Bethany had chopped off my finger to eat. But fish ate other fish—was that like me scraping skin cells away when I scratched? Or… I couldn't think of a proper comparison. But we weren't part of Ocean. That was the point. It was different for us.

Another net was hauled overboard and dumped onto the deck. More writhing wriggling gasping fish, of more different sorts and types. We knew next to nothing about the fish that lived in Ocean. They avoided the Centre, and even Communicators didn't go swimming around in many other parts of Ocean, and at any rate we stayed on the surface. In the last half a minute I had learnt more about Ocean's fish than I ever had before. Ocean's dying fish, dying right here in front of me when I could save them.

Except I couldn't, could I? If I threw them back overboard, I'd be thrown back overboard myself, and they wouldn't haul me out again this time, either. And then they'd just hoick more fish back up again. I couldn't win this one.

But I could watch, and find out what was actually happening. I could look at the people doing it, not just the fish, and see what they thought they were doing.

Surviving. They think they're surviving, said a little voice at the back of my head.

You couldn't live on that damned vegetable soup.

I looked around at the people working the nets, as the third net came over the railings. I don't know what I was expecting. Some kind of vicious joy, perhaps? Some sort of rejoicing that they were breaking the Contract, that they were running their own lives or whatever the hell it was they thought they were doing. Satisfaction, perhaps.

There was that satisfaction when I looked. Satisfaction in a job achieved, satisfaction that they were feeding themselves and their children. Another day gone, another meal provided. I swallowed back a return bout of that nausea at the idea of actually eating the bodies that lay in front of me. But then, I'd only been eating weak vegetable soup for a day. I didn't have to make that decision, between starvation and eating Ocean's fish.

Not yet, anyway.

"We too are part of the ocean," Bethany said, next to me.

I swung round and looked at xem. Xyr eyes were steady.

"The ocean's own eat the ocean's own," xe said. "We know little about the sea-creatures, but we do know that. Why should we not do the same?"

"Because we know better," I said, automatically. "Because we are different. Because we promised Ocean we wouldn't."

"*We* did not promise the ocean," Bethany said sharply. "That was promised for us. By Communicators, indeed."

"Not by me," I said, defensively, and xyr gaze narrowed sharply. "I mean, it was a long time ago."

"And perhaps it is time to rethink," Bethany said.

The nets were being emptied now, the fish no longer moving. Dead. I thought for a moment that I could hear Ocean growling inside me.

"You don't touch the water," I said.

Bethany's chin went up slightly. "It still burns us."

"But you eat the fish," I said.

"We purify the fish. And then we cook it. It's not the same as fresh water." But xe didn't quite meet my eyes as xe said it.

I didn't believe that they could purify it as well as all that. Mostly, maybe. But there was still going to be something of Ocean in there, surely? And Bethany knew it. So what was that doing to them? Were they, really, becoming part of Ocean? Like I'd been thinking about? Or was xe hiding problems in the community; illness, death?

"Even fresh water doesn't burn me," I said, and stepped down onto the deck. I don't quite know why I did it. The people now piling the fish up all turned and stared at me, standing there barefoot in a puddle of water.

"You are of the ocean," Bethany said calmly. "And yet you won't turn predator."

I shrugged, feeling suddenly foolish. "That isn't how we are with Ocean."

They ate, and couldn't touch the water. I could touch the water, but wouldn't eat. Both crossing that boundary, in our different ways, and succeeding.

"We must skin and gut the fish now," Bethany said abruptly, and my stomach turned again. Xe must have seen it in my face. Xe snorted. "Don't worry, foolish child, I am not about to ask you to do this thing. I am not entirely unreasonable. But I am needed. I will shut you back in your cabin."

My chin went up. "I can watch. I should watch. You want me to understand this, right? Otherwise you'd have chucked me straight back over the rail. You can't ask me to understand and yet not permit me to see the whole thing. If you believe it's right, it must *all* be right."

Bethany was the first one to drop xyr eyes, this time.

"Very well," xe said, and walked over to the pile of fish, rolling up xyr sleeves. For a moment, I wondered if that was a glint of silver I saw on xyr skin? Then xe squatted and took a knife and a pair of gloves that one of the others offered, and I couldn't see enough skin to tell.

It was a bloody business, as Bethany had suggested it would be. I regretted my decision almost immediately. But if I was here watching for Ocean and for the Communicators—if that was why I was here, or at the least, the thing I could do now that I was here—then I needed to watch, not to turn away.

And predation is bloody. If the idea I was chewing over about predators and energy cycles and so on had any value to it, it would not, could not, be bloodless. Could we co-exist within Ocean, rather than skating on top of it? Could this mess of fish parts and slime be part of that?

Once they were finished, they pulled up buckets of Ocean-water and sluiced over the decks, washing the fish parts and slime over the edge. Bethany beckoned me over to the railing.

"Look," xe said, pointing down into the water. A crowd of other water-beings gathered just under the surface, jaws snapping at the stuff that was raining down on them. "They are of Ocean, and they happily eat it. That is what it is, to be part of the system."

I watched until all the fish-refuse was gone.

AT DINNER EVERYONE ATE TOGETHER,

on the big forward deck of the largest boat in the fleet. It was crowded, and Bethany and I squeezed in at the back, against the bulkhead of the central cabins. I could smell the fish in the stew that they ate; though once again, Bethany handed me a bowl of that same thin vegetable stew. Xyr sleeves were back down now, so I couldn't look again for that glint of silver. What was eating the fish doing to them here?

"You would be welcome to share our other food," xe said politely, but I shook my head.

I was really beginning to notice, though, that the vegetable stuff didn't fill me up. There was no way they could survive out here on only what they could grow on their own boats. None of the rest of us managed that. We relied on the protein from legumes on the farm-rafts; but those plants needed more space than they had here. Perhaps, in the longer run, they could begin to build their own rafts, but they couldn't grow the bamboo for that here, either. Of course, they had come out here with enough space to fend for themselves. Before it sank.

Maybe Kira and Stel had found a way by now to haul it up again. I felt a sudden wave of something—home-sickness, perhaps, or just Kira-sickness—in my stomach, then snorted to myself. More likely just hunger. I did wonder, though, what Kira would be making of all of this, if xe were here.

Which was a good point. Why wasn't xe here? Ocean had sent me here, just me. Why hadn't Ocean pushed the whole ship this way? Was Ocean expecting something of me? For the first time, I *wanted* to talk to Ocean, wanted to ask Ocean for explanations, to ask Ocean if the things I was just beginning to think could possibly be true. But I couldn't see any way to do that here without incurring the wrath of Bethany and the others. I wasn't at all sure they'd pull me out a second time. And I had no idea where my ship was now, and no trust that Ocean would bring me back to it. Nevertheless, I wished I could ask Ocean. I felt adrift, unsure of what I should be doing, and I didn't like it at all.

The empty bowls were being collected and stacked for cleaning. The noise of conversation was rising, then, through it, I heard it. Music, coming from the front of the boat. Just warming up, from the sound of it, but... Music. A flute. I missed my flute, suddenly, far more fiercely than I'd been missing Kira.

Bethany noticed me noticing.

"You like music?"

"It's what I'm going..." I stopped. I couldn't say the same thing I always said. I was stuck, now. "It's what I was going to do, before," I said instead, and clenched my teeth.

Bethany tipped xyr head slightly to one side. "Come, then," xe said, and led me forward.

As we went toward the place in the bow where the musicians had wedged themselves, a drum and something guitar-like joined in with the flute. No vocalists, though, not yet; this was a dancing-tune, not a song, even if no one was dancing.

There were four of them, once we got close enough that I could see. One with a four-string ukulele, one with a flute, one with a very shallow drum, and someone who I guessed was waiting to sing. The tune they were playing right now wasn't one I recognised. Not only that, it wasn't *like* anything I recognised. I mean, it was music, right enough. But—I sat myself down on the deck, listening. It wasn't tuned to the same scale I knew. And the rhythms were different, swinging differently, washing over me...

Ocean, I realised. It sounded of Ocean, and of the winds that blew through the boat. The music I played at home, the music we were all trained to, was what our ancestors had brought with them. Traditional. This was—this was something different. It was a merging of old Earth traditions and of the sounds of this world, the world that was ours now. I was aware that I might be overreacting, somewhere in the back of my head, as I listened with my mouth open. But this was *new*, and it felt right. It felt like it had when I'd floated on the surface of the water, and Ocean had finally spoken to me. However much I hadn't wanted that, it was wholly and undeniably of here. This too felt of here, not of the old world.

I felt tears starting in my eyes, and blinked them back fiercely. The synthesis I had been thinking of, back on the ship. The joining of two worlds. *This* was how that should sound. This music was telling me that story. Why had I not thought of that? I'd called myself a musician, and then thought I had to be a Communicator instead; but did I really have to be just one or the other?

Music could communicate. Why had it never occurred to me—to anyone—that the Communicators should be communicating not just with Ocean, but with everyone else as well. Could this be part of it? Part of joining ourselves to this world? My fingers itched to borrow their instruments, to listen to the tuning of the strings, the reverberation of that strange drum.

They finished the dancing-tune, and began a song. The hairs rose up on my arms as I listened. It wasn't one of the traditional songs I knew; not even one of the few new songs that told of our own time on this planet but in Old Earth style. The singer was telling the story of these people, of their setting off from Endeavour, full of excitement and expectation, of the hard work of the first months working to establish their little island; then of the storm and destruction, the failure of the island, everyone leaving on small boats with whatever they could grab. A single, soft, verse told of the meeting that decided what they would do next; of watching most of the islanders sail away, back to Endeavour, and of the few that chose to remain and see what they could do out here. The singer described their attempts to survive, as it became clearer that they could not; and then of the realisation that there was another option. The song ended not exactly triumphant, but hopeful.

What it did not do, at any point, was talk about Ocean, or about the Contract that they had broken. I frowned, and pulled myself reluctantly away from just appreciating the music.

"Is that what most of you think, then?" I asked Bethany. "That this was simply a survival decision, a sensible realisation of the possibilities of all that water and its inhabitants?"

"It was that," Bethany said. Xyr eyes flickered. "But not just that, I agree," xe added, reluctantly.

"Did that even come into anyone's thoughts, when you decided?" I demanded. "Did anyone *talk* about our responsibilities to Ocean?"

"I did, as it happens," Bethany said. "And not me alone, either. We are not *stupid*, child. We knew very well that we would be facing opposition, that if Endeavour found out, they would come after us."

"What do you mean, if?" I asked. "You must have known that Ocean would tell us."

Bethany snorted. "You assume that people still believe that."

I blinked at xem. Though for certain it shouldn't have surprised me, after what Kira had been saying. "You mean, people don't *believe* that Ocean is, is…"

"Is Ocean? Is sentient? No, child, they don't. The Communicators have hardly done their job there."

"So… Everyone thought it was just about safety, or, or some old taboo that no longer held water," I said slowly. "They thought that the time was come for new ideas, and for surviving out here."

"For surviving out here as part of the planet, not holding ourselves aloof," Bethany said.

"I didn't notice you hurrying to put your feet in that water," I said, a little snidely.

Bethany shrugged. "I'm a realist, too, child. If I'm right, if we do need to merge these ecosystems, then it'll be the younger ones that it works for."

I really wanted, again, to check xyr skin.

"Hasn't happened yet," I said. "We've been here for, what, a century and a half?"

"But we haven't tried," Bethany said. "We've gone to such pains to stay separate. And yet you must have noticed that there are more Communicators in your generation than there are two generations above you."

I didn't say anything.

"Something is changing. But no one sitting around in that Centre, pontificating at one another, has thought of what that might mean. Of whether *we* might, after all, be changing."

"I wanted to leave," I said. "I never wanted to be a Communicator. I was nearly out, as well, when Ocean spoke to me last week. Two days before my birthday." I scowled. "Stuck with it, now."

"Well, you're not," Bethany said, mildly. "You can leave." Xe looked straight at me. "You could stay here. You could help us make this change. I've seen *you*, watching today. You think like us. You think we need to be part of this planet, not separate from it. You could come with us."

I sat and thought about it. The musicians were still playing.

If I stayed, I wouldn't have to be a Communicator any more. Would I still be *able* to communicate with Ocean? I wanted not to care about that, but at the same time, I wanted, so badly, to know what Ocean thought of all this. What Ocean expected of me here. I couldn't say that to Bethany. I could barely say it to myself.

If I stayed, they'd send someone else out to look for the fleet, soon enough. They couldn't expect to get away forever. Could they? Was the planet that big? Would Ocean help?

What did Ocean want? Why had Ocean brought me here?

Bethany had wandered off, while I sat thinking. Xe came back, holding a bowl.

"If you believe that I'm right," xe said quietly, "if you want to join us. If you want to help us. You should eat this."

I looked at the bowl. Fish. Fish stew.

I could smell it, rich and Ocean-smelling. A part of my hindbrain told me very clearly just how good this was; that this was what my body needed.

Another part told me just how bad of an idea this was. It was *forbidden*. It was—it was *forbidden*, that was all there was to it. Kira would be disgusted. Alren would be horrified. Everyone would be horrified. You couldn't eat fish; you just couldn't.

Did I believe what I'd been starting to think, what Bethany had been saying? Did I believe it enough? What did Ocean really want of us?

Tentatively, slowly, I put my hand out towards the bowl.

Then I saw Kira, in my mind's eye; saw xyr look of horror; saw the mistrust xe had shown me back on the ship turn to horrified disgust, and my throat closed up.

I pulled my hand back.

"I can't do it," I said, looking down at my hands. "I'm sorry. I just can't."

Bethany's hands weren't unkind as xe pulled me to my feet and marched me back to that little cabin to be locked in. They weren't unkind. But they were implacable.

SHUT IN THAT CABIN ON my own, I didn't have much option but to think everything over again.

The problem was… The problem was, I thought Bethany was right. It made me really seriously uncomfortable, but I thought xe was right. We weren't living here, not really; we were just kind of hovering over Ocean's surface. We couldn't carry on like this. Well. We *could*, probably. A hundred years and change; we'd found sustainability, albeit a bit precarious. But precarious—and limiting—was exactly what it was. Fundamentally, we were living much like we were still in space than like we were on a planet.

Which didn't make any sense. We were here for good. Shouldn't we act like it? Which had to mean change, of some sort.

I found myself humming one of the tunes from earlier. Music that was building on the old ways, the ways we'd been painstakingly maintaining for the last hundred years; but which also changed, reflecting where we are now. Music that had both Ocean and humanity in it.

Mixing Ocean and humanity together. They were doing that here, but only halfway. Water made them unwell, still, or they thought it did. But if they could eat the fish... could it just be thinking?

The *idea* of fish made me nauseous, but if Bethany and everyone else here could eat it, chances were it wouldn't actually make me sick, if I could bring myself to try.

We distilled our water, and we breathed the air without worrying, because the water in that was, effectively, distilled too. But could there be something in there that survived that process? Something that was slowly bringing us closer to Ocean? Something that our scientists hadn't spotted before the Contract, because it didn't make us ill, and had been prevented from spotting since then by Communicators trying to enforce the contract. Because like they kept telling Delas, experimenting on Ocean without Ocean's consent was not permissible, and no one wanted to ask Ocean for consent.

But even if there was something in all of that, what they were doing here, the fishers, was without Ocean's permission or consent, and that couldn't be right.

What if Ocean gave permission, though? What if...?

I swallowed. I'd been asking myself, why me? Why did Ocean tell me? Why did Ocean bring me here? And something else had been niggling at the back of my mind, something really basic I'd been taught at the Centre right from the start. Ocean didn't speak to us directly, not in words, like another human. What Ocean said to us was mediated by our own minds. Did that also mean, by our own beliefs and expectations? Ocean had told me that there were people eating fish, and I'd been horrified at the breach of the Contract. But was that what *Ocean* had felt about it? Could Ocean have meant to convey a different message, after all?

My thoughts stuttered to a halt as I heard voices, the other side the bulkhead behind me.

"Chuck 'em overboard," said one voice, "and be done with it."

"I think there's still hope; it's a big taboo to over-come." That was Bethany.

The other voice snorted. "And meanwhile? We've got a Communicator on board. They're going to be looking for us harder than ever."

"We've got a *hostage*," Bethany said.

"If they let us get close enough to tell 'em," a third voice said.

"If they think we've got xem, they'll be after us either way," Bethany said.

"Yeah, well, maybe, and maybe we just shouldn't take chances."

The voices faded away.

So now I had to worry—again—about whether Bethany could prevent me from going over the side. Great.

What was I going to do, anyway? I had all these huge terrifying ideas, all these wild speculations, but they were just that, speculations. I was a sixteen-year-old brand new Communicator who had gotten myself lost. I wasn't in a position to do—well, anything. And I didn't know anything. Terrified though I was of the idea—what if I were wrong, but worse, what if I were right?—I had to talk to Ocean. I had to see whether these ideas I was having were anything to do with what Ocean wanted. And then, even if they were, I needed to get back to the ship and to Comm Alren. Not that Comm Alren was likely to be convinced by anything I had to say. But if I were right, I had to *try*.

And anyway, what was the alternative? Wait to be rescued? Sit on board here until they got fed up and threw me overboard? Take Bethany's offer and keep running with them? They were going to get caught eventually.

I could go overboard myself now, and take my chances. Ocean had brought me here, without telling me anything—or maybe just without telling me anything I'd been able to hear. Either way, Ocean could damn well talk to me, and then Ocean could take me away again.

Even knowing I was a Communicator, they hadn't thought about the porthole. It was small. It was right in the stern of the boat. You couldn't climb out of here without falling straight into Ocean. So no one could get out,.

No one who wasn't happy to fall straight into Ocean.

It wasn't ideal. There was the risk that the undertow of the boat's passage would pull me straight under. But the wind was light, and we were moving slowly; and at the stern, I wouldn't be run over.

There was also the risk that Ocean wouldn't talk to me, wouldn't help me, and I'd drown as soon as I ran out of energy. Which, after a day of short rations following my first attempt at nearly drowning, wouldn't take that long. But surely Ocean wouldn't waste all the trouble it had gone to in getting me here. Would it? Ocean didn't think like a human. Maybe Ocean wouldn't care.

Anyway. I was fed up, and I was done with sitting around chewing my nails and waiting and wondering. I wanted answers, and I wanted out.

The sun had already mostly set. Ocean looked dark and cold through the porthole. I reminded myself that Ocean was never truly cold; I reminded myself of how much time I had spent just floating around aimlessly in Ocean.

Ocean might not speak to me. Or hear me. Ocean might not actually drown me, just set out to ignore me until I drowned all of myself.

But I was *done* with being tugged around in the undertow of everyone else. Kira, Comm Alren, Bethany... I was going to make a decision of my own for once.

The porthole was easy enough to open. It was harder getting through it—I'm skinny (Kira would have had a much worse time of it) but it was a tight fit nonetheless, and my vest got ripped on the way through with a scrape down my side as well. But I wriggled myself feet-first all the way out, then my shoulders last of all, hands still holding onto the top of the porthole, my fingers beginning to cramp. It looked a lot further down from here, dangling with my feet over the water, than it had from safely inside the cabin. Not that I had any option, now; there was no way I could turn around and get back in there.

I took a deep breath, brought my feet up onto the hull, and let go, pushing off as hard as I could with my feet, trying to get as far away from the boat as I could. I leaped, tumbled over backwards, and entered the water head-first with my arms cleaving Ocean's water.

THE SUN VANISHED BELOW THE

horizon as the fleet sailed away from me. For a while, I just floated, listening to the sound of the water in my ears, watching the stars appear as the last glow in the sky faded. They were as bright as I'd ever seen them. The water was soft and comforting against my skin. I felt it lapping against my clavicle; air and water meeting with me suspended at the junction between them.

Ocean bubbled in my ears; and I spoke to Ocean. I spoke of ecosystems. I spoke of the agreement that was made before, and whether it was time to change this agreement. I spoke of distance, and of people who no longer understood what Ocean was. I spoke of division, and I spoke of reuniting.

For the first time, I tried to really experience Ocean as a fellow sentient, however different Ocean might be from me. I spoke to Ocean as I would to a partner; to a friend.

Ocean didn't say anything, for a long while. But Ocean was there, still; I could feel Ocean's awareness. I felt the ripples of fish swimming past my fingertips in the darkness, and I wondered anxiously for a moment about that giant fish that Serah and I watched from the ship. Not much I could do about it, if I was about to be eaten. No point in worrying.

After a while, a little more tentatively, I asked if Ocean had any idea where *my* ship might be.

For a while, there was nothing. I floated, and thought.

I began to notice a gentle swell, washing me in one direction. Ocean was taking me somewhere. I had to hope it was where I wanted to be. Not much I could do about it. I floated, and watched the stars.

Ocean began to tell me a story, of my ancestors' arrival, of Ocean's bemusement as the great ships settled onto Ocean and floated. I got the sense that time didn't mean the same to Ocean as it did to me. I didn't know when Ocean had arisen as a sentience, but Ocean now was, if not quite immortal, potentially as long-lived as the planet. Human lives were brief flickers to Ocean.

So, humans arrived, and Ocean knew that there were beings of some sort, floating in (and then, later, on) the ships. New species had arisen in Ocean before. But these stayed out of the water, and Ocean could not speak to them. Ocean's puzzlement grew; and then these new things began to take other beings out of Ocean's water. They took, but nothing returned. Ocean was diminishing, very slightly, but diminishing. Something that had never happened before; everything in Ocean remained in Ocean, whatever form it might take at any given moment, or went and came back as water became rain. Ocean could potentially live as long as the planet, but Ocean was not immortal. Ocean discovered that Ocean could be shrunk.

(Our ancestors had wanted to save every bit of potential compost they could, for the plants. Everything went into the composters, big or small; nothing went back into the water.)

Ocean was distressed. Ocean tried to attract attention.

(Ocean destroyed a large chunk of Endeavour. That got attention, right enough.)

Then there was the first Communicator, the first human to find xemself able to swim in Ocean's water, the first human who listened when Ocean spoke to them. Ocean, distressed and angry, explained that Ocean was losing parts of Ocean-self.

The human promised to stop it, and Ocean accepted that. The humans had come into Ocean's water, now, and so they would be part of Ocean. All would be well. Ocean settled, to await that joining. Now that Ocean was no longer diminishing, Ocean had time.

But instead the humans remained on their floating ships, and they built more floating land, and, with a few exceptions, they stayed out of Ocean's water. On the other hand, they did not take any more of Ocean's fish. For a while, that sufficed. Ocean could be patient. Change was always gradual.

But Ocean began to realise that there *was* no change here; that the humans remained separate. This was not what Ocean wanted. Ocean tried to talk to the Communicators, but they seemed unable to understand. Then Ocean expressed its displeasure. (Gennaro, I thought, and suppressed a wince.) And still there was no comprehension. Then Ocean found, finally, humans that were beginning, albeit imperfectly, to join with Ocean. (I realised that this had to mean that as well as eating fish, Bethany's people must have been both returning the leftovers to Ocean, and sending human bodies into Ocean. It made sense both that they would have had deaths, and that they would have had no other way of dealing with the bodies; no room to compost. It made sense, but it was hard not to shudder at the thought, even if it was what Ocean wanted.)

Ocean found these people, and Ocean found a mind that felt different among the humans who swam, and it tried to convey the message that we should learn from these humans. And when that seemed not to work, Ocean brought the mind to them.

(It was a heady feeling, that moment of confirmation, of Ocean agreeing—more or less—with me. It feels good, to be right. Ocean, too, seemed oddly satisfied with Ocean-self as Ocean told me the story.)

Something began to intrude itself upon my awareness; a different note in the water sloshing in my ears. I rolled over in the water so I could lift my head up out of the water and look around; and there, halfway between me and the horizon, was the ship, lit up like a beacon. I began paddling towards it.

Ocean had explained to me. Now I had to explain to the others, what it was that Ocean wanted. That was, after all, the job of a Communicator. Even if in this particular instance, what Ocean wanted was going to be, well... moderately unpopular, to say the least. But Alren was a Communicator too. With actual experience, unlike me.

Alren would understand what I had realised, once I'd explained that we'd been misunderstanding things. Allowing our preconceptions to affect what we thought we heard. Alren would understand that we had to work with Ocean. And then Alren could sort everyone else out.

My part was nearly over, I told myself, as I paddled wearily towards the ship.

Nearly done.

THERE WAS A LOT OF fuss, initially, and I didn't get to say anything at all for a while. Comm Alren bundled me into my bed in my cabin. Kira fussed over me, and got told off by Comm Alren and burst into tears and got terribly embarrassed and left again.

Serah didn't fuss. Serah stood nearby, eyes cold, and said nothing.

Clean dry clothes were found for me and someone brought me food. More soup, but ours had real grains in and lentils. I ate it thankfully, washed down with an infusion.

"So," Serah said, once I was scraping out the bottom of the bowl. "Where have you been? Even a Communicator cannot surely survive afloat for two full days."

"In fact..." Alren began, but Serah waved xem to silence without looking over.

"I was in the water," I said, before Alren and Serah could start arguing, "as Comm Alren had suggested, and I was caught in a current and swept away from the ship. None of you heard me calling." Alren took a breath, and I hastily added "I think—I'm sure—Ocean took me. Deliberately."

Serah tipped xyr head slightly to one side. Alren was frowning. Neither of them interrupted.

"I knew, it was Ocean, but to be honest, I didn't think I'd make it. I didn't know why it was happening."

"Did you ask Ocean?" Alren asked.

I shrugged. "Sure. Ocean wasn't talking. So I floated, and then eventually a little boat saw me and hauled me out of the water. And warmed me up and fed me and gave me somewhere to sleep."

Serah's face was still blank, but I was fairly sure xe knew where I was going with this.

"I spent yesterday with them," I said. "There was a whole fleet of small boats, not a large fleet, maybe a dozen. They had growing-trays on board, but only enough for veg and greens, so at first I thought they must be on a long voyage. Then, eventually, I realised that they were the fleet we were after. The... fishers."

There was an audible intake of breath from my listeners at the word.

"They say that they can't survive without protein, and they can't grow protein off the back of a little boat. Not even off several little boats."

"Then they should come back to Endeavour," Serah said grimly.

"And then they'd be right at the bottom of the heap," I said. "They took their chance, and Gennaro sank, and it wasn't their doing, but their old homes aren't there any more either."

I had to tell them about Ocean, but I could feel myself putting it off. It had all seemed so clear, so simple, when I was in Ocean, but now I was here, in front of Alren, I had a rising anxiety about how xe would react.

"So they break the Contract instead," Alren said. "Jennery, you sound disturbingly sympathetic to these reprobates."

"They don't believe in the Contract." I raised my voice in frustration. "That's the point. More and more people don't believe in the Contract." Alren tried to say something, but I kept talking. I needed to talk about Ocean, yes, but it was important that Alren and Serah understand this too. And it would lay the foundations for talking to them about Ocean. "The Communicators have shut themselves—ourselves—off in the Centre. No one talks to us properly. No one listens to us properly. More and more people think that Ocean is a myth, that the Contract is foolish. People living in Endeavour."

"I don't know where you get your ideas from..." Alren started, shaking xyr head disapprovingly, but Serah interrupted xem.

"Jennery is correct," xe said. "And we have spoken of this to you. Many times."

"Well, it is your job to *fix* this," Alren snapped. "And to enforce the Contract. Ours is to speak with Ocean."

I felt sick trying to argue with both of them, and me only just sixteen and barely a Communicator at all. But Ocean had spoken to me, not to them, and Ocean had taken me to the fishers, and if I didn't do it no one else was going to, and who knew what Ocean would do then. Our job was to speak with Ocean. *My* job.

"We've been on this planet over a hundred years," I said, before Alren and Serah could start arguing with each other. "And we're not leaving, right?"

"Leaving?" Alren asked.

"Going back to Old Earth," I said. "I don't know if anyone thought that, back when the Contract came about, but it's not going to happen, right? We can't leave ourselves, because our ship is an island now. And no one's coming to get us. This is our planet now."

Serah was staring at me intently, a small frown between xyr eyebrows. Alren was shaking xyr head slightly. But they let me speak.

"So why are we living on it like, like we're temporary?" I asked. My voice wobbled. I had to make them understand. I had to get them to realise what Ocean meant. And I was still terrified of saying that I'd spoken to Ocean, that *my* interpretation of Ocean was the right one, over all these people at the Centre with more experience than me. But if I could make them see it first, maybe then Alren would accept it. Would be able to hear it for xemself. I had to change xyr ideas before xe could hear it from Ocean.

"We're perched on top of Ocean, like a little bubble. Entirely outside Ocean's ecosystem. Why?"

"Because Ocean's ecosystem would make us ill," Alren said, rolling xyr eyes. "When we landed, we intended to change it, but the discovery of Ocean's sentience prevented that. You know this, Jennery."

"We can't change Ocean," I agreed, "Not without Ocean's consent. But why can't we change *us*?"

Alren opened xyr mouth, looking annoyed, and I barrelled on before xe could speak.

"We're changing already," I said. "There are more Communicators now than there used to be, right? More people can tolerate the water. More people speaking to Ocean. We're *changing*. People get splashed now and they don't worry about it. Back when Endeavour landed, that would have burned humans, even the smallest drops. Because we're *changing*. When was the last time someone died at the Testing? We're *changing*. Ocean has an ecosystem. Ocean doesn't mind if one thing eats another thing." I was talking faster and faster now, about to say it, and surely now they would, Alren would, understand. "Ocean just wants everything to *be* part of that ecosystem. That's what Ocean said. When Ocean spoke to me. When I asked Ocean. That's what Ocean *told* me. Why can't we change?"

Alren's eyes went wide, then xe frowned deeply. I stared anxiously at xem, trying to work out what xe was thinking.

"Is that what these law-breakers are doing?" Serah asked, after a long moment.

"They're surviving," I said, pulling my attention away from Alren. "They're purifying the fish, as best they can, but I don't think it's perfect, I can't believe they're set up like Endevaour was before the Contract—and yet they're surviving." I paused. I was feeling very tired, all of a sudden, but I tried to sit up a bit more, tried to pull my arguments back together. "Think. Think about how crowded Endeavour is, how precarious we are. We're one crop failure away from starvation. These people are surviving on the greenery they grow on the back of a bunch of tiny little boats, and the fish from Ocean."

"Jennery, this is absurd," Alren said briskly. "I don't know what you imagined Ocean said to you but I fear it must have been brought on by your long time in the water. You are very new to this, after all."

"But…" My stomach lurched. Alren wasn't *listening*. I hadn't imagined anything. I hadn't! Why wouldn't xe *listen*? I tried to pull my thoughts together, but my head felt fuzzy, and the words wouldn't come.

"The fishers have broken the law," Serah said, looking away. "These hypotheticals are for another time. Perhaps you should discuss this with the other Communicators back on Endeavour. We cannot change our orders now. If you can add nothing more, I will continue the search." Xe turned on xyr heel and left. My stomach twisted.

"Alren, I spoke to Ocean, really, you need to listen, you need to speak to Ocean, yourself, you have to listen…" I turned to xem, pleading, trying to find the words to explain about preconceptions, but I couldn't make a sentence come together, the ideas sliding away from me like fish, flopping and gasping in the net of my head..

My eyelids were getting heavier, impossibly heavy, despite my best efforts. That tea…?

"I think it's best you sleep now," Alren said, as I drifted out of consciousness, fighting it all the way.

WHEN I WOKE UP AGAIN, thick-mouthed and fuzzy-headed, the cabin was empty. I could hear a lot of shouting and tramping around above my head. I hesitated for a moment, then rolled out of the bunk, pulled on some clothes, and went up to the deck.

Halfway between us and the horizon, I saw the fleet. We were visibly closing on them, our sails up and straining in the wind. My heart sank.

Serah was talking to the other cops. One of xem was stringing a bow, the others already held xyrs in xyr hands. My heart sank further still. Shit. Had things got that far already? Alren was up by the helm, staring out at the fleet. I ran forward and up the steps to reach xem.

"What are you *doing*?" I asked, then belatedly realised that I could almost certainly have been more polite.

"What we came here to do," Alren said crisply.

"But they've got their bows out down there! Shouldn't we be giving the fleet a chance before we *shoot* at them?"

"Serah hailed them already," Alren said. "They have not chosen to come quietly. We have to be seen to enforce the rules, Jennery. Ocean must see us enforce the rules."

"Ocean doesn't *want* us to enforce the rules!" I shouted. "That's what I've been trying to tell you! You're not listening to me, and you're not listening to Ocean."

We were getting closer to the fleet. All the boats had as much sail up as they could cram on, and I could see people frantically pulling at the sheets to adjust the trim, to squeeze out as much speed as they could, but they had no hope of outrunning us now.

"Jennery," Alren said. "I don't say you don't believe what you're saying, but you must understand that you are very young and inexperienced. For pity's sake, you only spoke to Ocean for the first time, what, four days ago? You had a traumatic experience, *several* traumatic experiences, those people over there doubtless did their best to poison your mind, and it is hardly surprising that you might imagine things. That your state of mind might affect your experience of Ocean's communication."

"I wasn't imagining anything," I said. "I'm not *stupid*. When was the last time you communicated with Ocean? Have you even tried to check since I got back and told you?"

Alren's back stiffened. "I communicate regularly, as you know. I have not received anything like the information you describe."

"That's because you're not *listening*," I repeated, furious. "Because you think you already know what Ocean's saying. I'm not the one whose state of mind is affecting their communication, you are. There's a *reason* Ocean is speaking to someone who hasn't been at this for years."

Alren was just as angry now as I was. "I am sorry, Jennery, but…"

"They're going to *shoot*," I wailed. "Stop them! Go into Ocean and just *listen*!"

"If these people cooperate, they have nothing to fear."

From further down the ship, I heard Serah's voice boom out of a speaking-trumpet.

"For the last time! Come about and hove to immediately and we will not harm you."

I didn't see any reaction from the fleet—no one looking round, no one letting out a sail. I didn't expect to; if they were desperate enough to be here in the first place, they were desperate enough to keep trying to get away. Also, I wouldn't have believed Serah either.

The ship heeled over, and I nearly fell. The waves had begun to pick up. I looked around. Enormous dark clouds were coming across the sky towards us at an uncanny rate. My pulse rocketed. I saw one of

Serah's cops turning to look over xyr shoulder, xyr expression anxious.

The ship pitched, and a wave sloshed over the coaming. I was leaning right there, and it soaked me from the shoulders down.

And as the water hit me, I knew what Ocean was doing. We were all screwed.

"SHIT, SHIT, ALREN, YOU HAVE to STOP!" I shrieked, but Alren wasn't listening any more, fighting the wheel with concentration as the wind began to increase.

The air was buffeting me ever more strongly, and it was full of water, the wind blowing spray up towards us as the waves crashed onto the ship. The waves were a different colour, too, from Ocean's usual pale green; darker, more menacing somehow, and it tasted sour. I could feel Ocean's distress and fury as though it were my own, and the knowledge of my failure rocked me backwards. I had to fix this. I had to get someone to listen—to me, and to Ocean.

I turned to look down at the main deck. One of Serah's officers was on the floor, wet from head to toe, clutching at xyr leg, xyr face agonised. Knocked over by that same wave that had spoken to me, unless I missed my guess. Serah xemself was leaning into the railing, fighting to stay upright. I couldn't see xyr face from here—xe was facing out towards the fleet—but everything about xyr body language spoke of purpose and determination.

I followed the direction of xyr gaze towards the fleet. They were barely visible, just glimpses of hull and mast and flashes of dark faces, through the spray and waves leaping between here and there. My eyes jerked back to Serah. xe raised xyr bow, sighting carefully, and my stomach lurched. Then another wave hit us, fully broadside, and I was on my arse on the deck, swearing. When I scrambled up again, Serah was still upright, still facing out, but the bow was flat across the railing as xe clung on with both hands.

I hoped desperately that Serah hadn't been able to get a shot off before the wave. But I was more focussed now on the fact that, quite clearly, we were all going to die.

"Alren!" I screamed again, and pulled myself upwards and towards xem. Xe was clinging to the wheel with all xyr strength.

"Jennery, for goodness' sake," Alren snapped. "Whatever you have to say I cannot imagine it is going to be helpful right now."

"Can't you *tell*?" I half-shouted, to be heard over the roar of the waves and the wind, my voice fighting against it. "It's Ocean, Alren. Ocean is doing this, and Ocean is *really pissed off.*"

"We are *trying* to despatch our duties," Alren said, then swore, words I had never heard xem use, fighting an enormous wave that was pushing us away from the fleet.

"How obvious does it have to be? Ocean doesn't *want* you to dispatch your duties!" I said. "For fuck's sake, Alren, you're a *Communicator.* If Ocean were any thicker in this air we wouldn't be breathing, we'd be bloody drowning." I took a breath and proved my own point by nearly choking on a handful of spray—almost a wave in its own right—that blew into my face. "If you won't believe me, will you believe Ocean? Will you listen? Really listen, not think you know what you're hearing because it's what the damn Contract says?"

Alren stared at me, then at the violence of the water around us. Xe freed a hand and, hesitantly, reached out to catch a handful of spray. Xe clenched xyr hand around it, and xyr eyes widened. Hope rose suddenly, shockingly, inside me.

"Jennery," xe said. "Take the wheel. Hold this course. You hear me? You must hold this course."

I didn't have to. I could turn us away from the fleet myself. But Alren had to come to this xemself, or it would be all to do again. I took the wheel, and was immediately struck by how *strong* Alren must be. It was as much as I could do to stay on my feet. I set my body-weight against it, and held on grimly.

Alren, like me a few minutes before, was plastered against the coaming. A wave hit xem full on. Xe shuddered and gasped, looking for a moment just like those fish on the deck of the fleet. I thought then of the soup, and stifled an unwelcome nausea.

It seemed to take an eternity, while I battled with the wheel, growing steadily more weary of holding that damn stupid course. I didn't dare to look down towards Serah and the other cops. If they did, somehow, get a shot off, if someone was hurt, or killed, would it all be fucked entirely?

It seemed to take an eternity; but it was probably only a minute, no more.

"Jennery!" Alren called, finally, xyr eyes wide and face shocked. "Steer to port. Steer *away*. Away! Now!"

Tears started in my eyes, mingling with the Ocean-spray, the relief part of me and of the water at the same time, as I did as I was told.

THE SHIP HEELED SHARPLY AS I pulled the helm over to port. The wind was still howling, the waves were still smashing against the ship. But we were steering away now, the waves coming at us stern-first rather than broadside, so we were no longer about to be swamped entirely at any moment. Braced against the coaming, Alren still stood white and strained-looking.

Serah was climbing the ladder from the main deck, naked fury on xyr face.

"What in the hells do you think you are doing," xe hissed. "Turn around *immediately*, Jennery. Alren, what are you *doing*, allowing this idiot to steer us away? We must go *back*, we must *deal* with this."

"We must not," Alren said flatly.

Serah swore in a tirade of expletives, some of which I'd never even heard before. I was impressed.

"We must not," Alren repeated, after Serah ran out of steam. "I have Communicated, Serah. I have listened to Ocean, finally, properly, and," a tiny wince crossed xyr face, "Jennery is right. Look at this storm. *Look at it*. Ocean does not want you to *deal with* these people. Ocean wants something else."

"This is absurd," Serah hissed. Xe stood at the top of the ladder now, bracing xemself on the railing. "You think you have authority here…"

"I do have authority here," Alren said.

"Not sole authority," Serah said, and my stomach churned slightly as I tried to work out what exactly xe could mean. "If I have reason to believe that there is a *problem* here…"

"Serah. Comm Alren." Stel had come to the bottom of the ladder. "I have—you might want to hear this." Kira stood behind Stel looking anxious.

Serah was still wild-eyed. At least the storm was calming as we sailed further from the fleet.

"Come up," Alren said. Xe stared at Serah until Serah, grudgingly, moved away from the top of the ladder to make room for Stel.

The space up by the helm was getting crowded now. Serah stood against the railing on the windward side of the ship, the heel of the ship raising xem slightly higher than the rest of us. Spray was still coming aboard with the wind, not that it mattered much given how damp we all were already. Stel stepped away from the top of the ladder once xe was up, leaving just enough room for Kira to squeeze up behind. Kira was fiddling with xyr wet hair, xyr eyes wide.

"We've been looking into why the island sank," Stel began.

Serah waved an impatient hand. "Yes, yes, get to the point."

Stel huffed an irritated breath through xyr nose, went to fold xyr arms, then thought better of it and grabbed for the rail again as the ship lurched slightly. "Well then. Ocean sank it."

"*What*?" Serah said.

Alren didn't look surprised. Which was a relief; it meant xe must have got much the same story from Ocean as I had, once xe had finally started paying attention. Ocean had been trying to do something about this problem. Show Ocean's displeasure, create a crisis. It had been stupid of us to think that Ocean's calm quiescence over the past hundred years meant Ocean *couldn't* become angry again, or take action like before.

Stel shrugged, more relaxed now xe had delivered the news. "Yeah, surprised me too, Serah. But the results are pretty clear. There's only one problem with any of the parts we've found; the same thing, over and over again. Crucial pieces just eaten away. And by eaten, I mean actual teethmarks."

"So you believe that *Ocean* made that happen?" Serah said, derisive. Xe had stepped forwards slightly, away from the railing, crowding the rest of us more. "Surely this is just an accident, some unusual fish behaviour."

"The fish *are* Ocean," Alren said, xyr chin going up as xe turned slightly to face Serah. "Fish behaviour is Ocean behaviour."

"Never seen anything like it before," Stel said, and the other two turned away from one another to look back at Stel. "We've had bamboo rafts all over the planet for decades. Decades. This has *never* happened before.

So, like Comm Alren says, if the fish are Ocean, then this was Ocean. End of."

"Ocean sank Gennaro," Serah said. I couldn't interpret xyr tone. "Ocean killed people and made people homeless."

"And now Ocean is defending the remainder," Alren said.

Serah's teeth were gritted so tightly I could see the muscle bulging in xyr jaw. "Ocean *killed* people. How can you defend this situation, where we bow to Ocean, where we must not hurt Ocean but Ocean can hurt us with impunity..."

"Wait," I said, and everyone turned to look at me. "You were shooting at the fishers because they broke the Contract. But now you're saying you don't like the Contract. So why do you care what the fishers do?"

"It is the law," Serah said. "If we simply let people break it..."

"But you want to change the law," I interrupted. "That's what you're saying, right? You want to change the law so we don't have to defer to Ocean all the time? So that we do what we want?"

"And then we get drowned," Stel said, not quite under xyr breath.

"The people of Gennaro were abiding by the rules, and they still drowned," Serah snapped.

"Ocean wants to change the rules," I said.

Stel, Serah, and Kira all stared at me again. Alren was nodding, a little reluctantly maybe, but nodding. It gave me strength to keep going. That, and knowing that I had a responsibility to Ocean, and beyond that, to everyone else.

"That's what all this is about. Ocean doesn't like the way we're doing things. Ocean wants something different."

"And how would you know?" Serah asked.

"I'm a Communicator," I said. "I Communicate. I did *tell* you, yesterday, but no one," I gestured towards Serah and Alren, "was listening. Look. We made the Contract, and Ocean agreed to it, yeah. But I think— no, scrub that, I know—Ocean didn't expect it to work quite the way it did. I mean, we know Communicating with Ocean isn't exact, right? We know it has to work through us. I guess misunderstandings are inevitable, especially at the start." And in theory, having multiple Communicators was supposed to reduce the risk of error, but apparently the Communicators had backed themselves, ourselves, into thinking too alike. But now wasn't the time to go into that.

"And it seems like we're not wholly separate, right?" I said, instead. "More Communicators. That lot over there eating fish that can't possibly be wholly processed.

If Ocean, or the planet, or whatever, is changing us, if we're adapting to it, then something's crossing over." I thought of Delas, and that project xe'd never been given permission for. "Maybe it's time to let people properly look into what's going on, what happens with Communicators. But either way. We're all on the same planet. It's stupid to try to keep two ecosystems going, and Ocean doesn't even *want* us to."

They all looked at me, wide-eyed, and for a moment, no one said anything.

"Ocean drowned people, what, to get our attention?" Stel said slowly. Xe was frowning.

I bit my lip. Alren wouldn't like me saying this. "I think, maybe, the Communicators weren't able to hear what Ocean was saying. People are good at not hearing things they don't like, right?"

"I fear Jennery is right," Alren said abruptly, moving slightly to stand closer to me. "We will certainly have to think carefully about whether we have allowed ourselves to listen too much to ourselves, and not enough to Ocean. But then, perhaps, as we make this change, Communicators will no longer be necessary. We may all become Communicators."

I was feeling a new respect for Alren. Xe'd been a Communicator for decades. All of this had to hurt like hell. But xe was standing up for Ocean, and for me.

Serah was staring at both of us, that crease back between xyr eyebrows, xyr expression otherwise stern and unreadable. "You want us to change our whole way of being," xe said.

"Isn't that what you want too?" I asked. "But no, not really. Just to allow the separation to end. Slowly, maybe."

"And that starts by leaving the fishers alone?"

I shrugged. "Unless you want to go back into that storm and drown, yeah."

Serah scowled at me.

"We cannot change everything overnight," xe said.

"I'm not *suggesting* overnight," I said. "Gradually. I think Ocean understands gradual. Since it's, like, millions of years old or whatever."

Serah ignored me. "We cannot promise anything, from here. It is not within our power to make those sorts of decisions here and now."

"We could decide not to try to round up the fishers," I said, glaring at Serah.

"I think," Alren said, slightly drily, "that Ocean has made that decision for us. I am certainly not prepared to carry on risking this ship and everyone on it in that manner."

"No," Serah said. "The law is as it is. We are committed…"

Alren spoke over xem, more loudly. "As I said. I Communicated with Ocean myself, earlier, and I am confident that Jennery is correct. Now, we are going to continue to steer away from the fishers. And Serah and I will talk."

I WANTED TO STAY FOR Serah and Alren's conversation, but Alren shooed me away, handing off the wheel to one of the crew. Grumpily, I went back down to the cabin. Sitting there by myself, I remembered with a sickening jolt that Serah and Co had those bows. And that thing Serah had said about mutiny… if Serah wasn't convinced after all, if Alren couldn't find a solution that Serah could buy into, what would happen then? Would the other officers point them at me, or at Alren, if it came down to it? Would Serah actually mutiny? Xe could claim that Alren had gone mad; could claim all sorts of things.

And then what—Serah would go for the fishers again, and Ocean would fight back again? And then if I hadn't been shot outright, I'd drown with everyone else. (Including Kira.) And everyone *else*, everyone back at Endeavour, would be back to square one. And if Ocean could sink Gennaro to make a point (could destroy that chunk of Endeavour, all that time ago), could it sink Endeavour and Alicante too? That would solve the problem; everyone would be folded back into Ocean, because everyone would be dead and rotting down in the deeps. From Ocean's point of view, that would be a success.

I don't know how long I sat there, my brain looping horrors, before the door opened and Alren came in.

"Serah and I have come to an agreement," xe said without preamble. "We will return to Endeavour without bothering the fishers further, and we will discuss all these matters in detail there. The Communicators, but also the city as a whole. This is not something that can be decided hastily. Or," xe sighed, looking suddenly unutterably weary, "on the basis of just your and my conversations with Ocean."

I was awash with relief. Bethany and the others were safe, at least for now.

"But," Alren said, and my shoulders tensed again. "Serah has one request. Well. One condition, rather. Someone must stay with the fishers. To watch them, and report back to them."

I looked at xem, my stomach tight.

Alren sat down opposite me. "I'm not going to make you do this. But you would be by far the best candidate. You must know that. You already know them. You understand what Ocean has been saying.

I opened my mouth to say no, then shut it again. What would Serah do, if I said no? What would happen to us here on this ship, to the fishers, to Ocean?

Alren rubbed at xyr eyes. "You are correct," xe said, "about the divide between us and the rest of the community. We need to fix that in Endeavour. But we also need to fix it, immediately, here. You've already started doing that, with these people." Xe shrugged. "But I cannot make you. Alternatively, we could ask the fleet to sail back to Endeavour with us, and find a volunteer there."

Would the fleet accept that, though? Or would they see it as a potential trap? And if they refused… it was straight back to the beginning.

But shouldn't I be back at Endeavour, putting Ocean's case? Otherwise there too it would be back to the beginning.

"I need to make people listen," I said. "Back home. None of you have been listening."

Alren nodded, looking down at xyr hands. Xe shut xyr eyes for a moment. "You are right, yes. We have not been listening. We have overwhelmed Ocean's communications with our own concepts. But," xe leant forwards, looked me in the eyes. "I promise you, Jennery, that I will make sure that this is understood. We have been letting Ocean down. We must not continue to do that. Whatever conclusions are reached, whatever way we find through this, we must not fail again to hear Ocean." Xe sat back again, and said, rather more sardonically, "And I fear we must both agree that I am in a better position than you are to get those set in their ways to listen."

It was true enough. Alren had the weight of age and experience that I didn't. I didn't like the sound of "finding a way through this" but I understood what Alren was saying.

The question was, did I trust xem? And, I found, I did.

I thought about staying on those tiny boats, instead of going back to my family and my city. I looked over at my gold shirt, hung on a peg, and missed Reth and Delas and even the brats so badly that I felt moisture in the corners of my eyes. But going back would also mean going back to the Centre. And who else would end up out here?

Did I really want to return to Endeavour? Badly enough to risk what might happen if I said no?

In my mind, I heard the musicians playing, and I thought of what I could learn from them.

"If I must," I said. "I'll do it. If I must."

I SAT, STARING INTO SPACE and not thinking at all, for a while after Alren left. Then I sighed, and rose to pack my belongings. Alren would have to go after the fleet again, or try to radio them, maybe, and it would take a little while to sort it all out. But they wouldn't want to hang around near us, once it was sorted.

I was just closing the bag when there was another knock on the door, but this time whoever it was waited for me to respond.

Kira. It was Kira, xyr eyes wide.

"Oh Jennery," xe said. "I'm so sorry!" Xe went to hug me, then hesitated, until I smiled at xem and put an arm around xem.

"For what?" I asked. The hug felt good.

Kira shrugged, not meeting my eyes. "What I said before. I was wrong. About Ocean. That's pretty obvious now, right? But, you, us, we *are* still friends, right? Even if I've been awful. Lecturing you about stuff. I'm sorry."

"It's all right," I said, surprised at how easy it was to say, and to mean. "It was—you were right, you know. About things needing to change. And hey, look! Things are changing." Probably. Hopefully. Slowly.

Kira snorted into my shoulder.

"And of course we're still friends." I smiled at xem, and xe finally met my eyes.

I don't know what I expected to see there. Real apology; understanding; and I saw both of those things, and it warmed me to my toes. But in my secret heart, maybe I did still want something more.

It wasn't there. It never had been. We were friends, and that was all Kira had ever wanted. It was me who'd thought of more. That hurt, sure, but it was okay. I'd cope. It wasn't fair to hold that against Kira. Xe didn't owe me anything.

"So," Kira said, after a moment. "What just *happened*?"

I sighed, and sat down on the edge of the hammock. "Ocean dragged me off to see the fishers. Ocean pulled me back here again afterwards. Ocean told me a whole load of things on the way."

"And Ocean drowned a whole island to get us here."

"Yeah," I said, wincing.

"I can't see why we want to do what Ocean says, if Ocean's prepared to just go around drowning people."

"Well, for one thing, because Ocean could drown all the rest of us if we don't," I said. "But—look, it just doesn't make sense to think about Ocean as a human person, Kira. Ocean is—Ocean is a planet. Or planet-sized, anyway. Ocean doesn't think the way we do. We can either get on with that, or we can leave; except we can't leave, can we?"

"Adapt or die," Kira said, slowly.

I shrugged. "Yeah, I guess so. But isn't that what humans are supposed to be good at? Adapting. We tried the other way around, remember, on Old Earth. We tried to adapt the planet instead of the humans. Didn't work out so well. Earth fought back. And Old Earth wasn't even sentient. We weren't listening to Ocean, and we weren't, we haven't been, letting ourselves be truly here. It's time to adapt properly, I guess."

Kira bit xyr lip. "I suppose so. I still can't help but be pissed off with Ocean, though."

I shrugged again. "That's fine. You don't have to be anything else. Actually, it's probably better to be pissed off with Ocean than to hold it too precious to be annoyed at, if you know what I mean? It's another being, like us, that we need to learn how to share a planet with, without just cutting ourselves off from each other. But also, you know, even if you're pissed off, it's my job to not be, now. Or at least, to try to understand. Even when other people don't have to. Right?"

Kira nodded. "You know what? Ocean, and the Communicators, are damn lucky to have you," xe said fiercely, and I laughed.

"What now, then? Are we all going back to Endeavour?"

"You are," I said. "I'm not." I explained the deal Alren and I had made.

"I'll miss you," Kira said, and threw xyr arms around me again.

Two weeks ago, even two days ago, I would have been ecstatic at this sign that Kira cared; would have been reading all sorts into it. Now, I just hugged xem back, and felt glad, deeply glad, that I had my friend back.

"I'll have a radio," I said. "Call me up when I'm in range. I'll tell Alren to let you know." I hugged xem a bit tighter. Xe still smelt good, smelt of Kira. "I'll miss you, too." Which was true. But... maybe it would be good to be a bit further away from Kira, for a while. After all. We'd still be friends when I got back.

Talking on the radio, though, even just occasionally, well; it would give me some sort of check on what Alren was telling me. If I listened carefully to what Kira said. It couldn't hurt. Even if I did trust Alren, I had a responsibility to Ocean. I had to make sure things went as they ought.

The door opened.

"Are you ready?" Alren said "It's time to go, Jennery."

"C'mon then, Kira," I said, letting go of Kira and picking up my bag. "You can wave me off."

"HELLO, COMMUNICATOR," BETHANY SAID, ONCE I was on the deck of the boat that had come to make the transfer.

"Jennery," I said. "It's Jennery."

"I gather you're here to keep an eye on us."

"Something like that," I said, and Bethany's lips twitched.

We were already sailing away, fast. I turned and gave a last wave to Kira.

When I turned back, Bethany was holding a half-full bowl, and a spoon.

"I thought you must be hungry," xe said. There was challenge in xyr eyes.

Small steps, small changes. I took the spoon.

JULIET KEMP LIVES IN LONDON

with their partners, child, and dog. Their novel *The Deep And Shining Dark* (Elsewhen Press) came out in 2018, and their short fiction has appeared in assorted magazines and anthologies. In their free time, they go bouldering, tend their towering to-be-read pile, and get over-enthusiastic about fountain pens. They can be found on Twitter at @julietk.

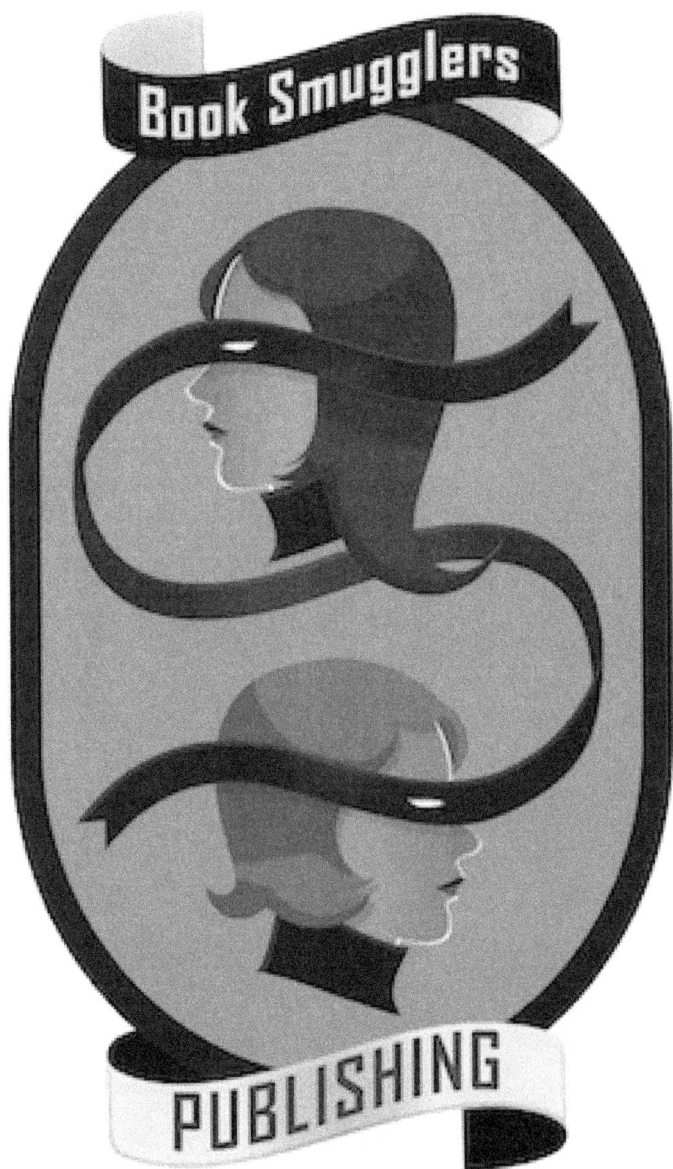

Book Smugglers

PUBLISHING

Visit www.booksmugglerspub.com for upcoming short stories, novels, and other publications

CPSIA information can be obtained
at www.ICGtesting.com
Printed in the USA
LVHW080930280920
667226LV00018B/2226

9 781791 381288